One of the shadows right along me had started to move. For seconds... that. But now there was certainly someone, a figure that seemed to have just risen out of the darkness. Then the figure glanced around. I immediately shrank back and put my torch away. It turned away again and started moving so fast it was practically running.

Where was it going? Of course, I had to follow it – even though the way it had just appeared out of the air made me certain that I was trailing a vampire.

I clutched my garlic tightly . . .

www.**randomhousechildrens**.co.uk

www.**petejohnsonauthor**.com

How many Pete Johnson books have you read?

## *Vampire stories*

THE VAMPIRE BLOG
*Winner of the Brilliant Book Award*
'A goodly dollop of fangly terror. Perfect' *The Bookbag*

THE VAMPIRE HUNTERS
'Packed full of adventure, comedy, laughs, intriguing characters
and a little bit of blood. This is a must read' *Scribbler*

THE VAMPIRE FIGHTERS
'Absolutely unputdownable' *Bookster Reviews*

## *Thrillers*

AVENGER
*Winner of the Sheffield Children's Book Award and the West Sussex Children's Book Award*
'Brilliant' *Sunday Express*

THE CREEPER
'Explores the subtle power of the imagination' *Books for Keeps*

EYES OF THE ALIEN
'Very readable with a skilful plot' *Observer*

THE FRIGHTENERS
'Prepare to be thoroughly spooked' *Daily Mail*

THE GHOST DOG
*Winner of the Young Telegraph / Fully Booked Award*
'Incredibly enjoyable' *Books for Keeps*

TRAITOR
'Fast-paced and energetic' *The Bookseller*

PHANTOM FEAR
*Includes:* MY FRIEND'S A WEREWOLF and THE PHANTOM THIEF

## *Funny stories*

THE BAD SPY'S GUIDE
*Shortlisted for the Blue Peter Book Award*
'This book grabs you from the first page' *Sunday Express*

HELP! I'M A CLASSROOM GAMBLER
*Winner of the Leicester Our Best Book Award*
'A real romp of a read that will leave readers ravenous for more' *Achuka*

HOW TO GET FAMOUS
*Winner of the Sheffield Community Libraries Prize*

HOW TO TRAIN YOUR PARENTS
'Makes you laugh out loud' *Sunday Times*

MY PARENTS ARE OUT OF CONTROL
'Glowing with Pete Johnson's trademark warmth and good humour' *Droplets of Ink*

RESCUING DAD
'Most buoyant, funny and optimistic' *Carousel*

THE TV TIME TRAVELLERS
'Another great humorous book from critically acclaimed Pete Johnson' *Literacy Times*

TRUST ME, I'M A TROUBLEMAKER
*Winner of the Calderdale Children's Book of the Year*

# THE
# VAMPIRE
# BEWITCHED

# Pete Johnson

CORGI YEARLING BOOKS

THE VAMPIRE BEWITCHED
A CORGI YEARLING BOOK 978 0 440 87014 2

First published in Great Britain by Corgi Yearling,
an imprint of Random House Children's Books
A Random House Group Company

This edition published 2014

1 3 5 7 9 10 8 6 4 2

Text copyright © Pete Johnson, 2014

The Random House Group Limited supports the Forest Stewardship Council®
(FSC®), the leading international forest-certification organisation. Our books
carrying the FSC label are printed on FSC®-certified paper. FSC is the only
forest-certification scheme supported by the leading environmental organisations,
including Greenpeace. Our paper procurement policy can be found at
www.randomhouse.co.uk/environment.

MIX
Paper from
responsible sources
FSC® C016897

Set in Century Schoolbook 12.5/16pt by Falcon Oast Graphic Art Ltd

Corgi Yearling Books are published by Random House
Children's Publishers UK, 61–63 Uxbridge Road, London W5 5SA

www.**randomhousechildrens**.co.uk
www.**totallyrandombooks**.co.uk
www.**randomhouse**.co.uk

Addresses for companies within The Random House Group Limited can be found
at: www.randomhouse.co.uk/offices.htm

THE RANDOM HOUSE GROUP Limited Reg. No. 954009

A CIP catalogue record for this book is available from the British Library.

Printed and bound in Great Britain by CPI Group (UK) Ltd, Croydon CR0 4YY

This story is dedicated to my nephew, Adam,
who thinks he'd make a cool half-vampire.

I think he would too!

# PROLOGUE

Someone is about to disappear.

Me.

By the time you read this I will have vanished. You might see my body roaming about, might even believe it's me, but it won't be. After tonight, the me who's writing this to you just won't exist any more.

I am under a slow-acting, but deadly spell. And there's nothing I can do to stop it. I am totally trapped.

All evening everyone's been expecting me to get hysterical and burst into tears. But I don't do crying. Not even now. And it isn't because I'm the least bit brave, but because all my tears are frozen inside me. I'm still numb with shock and terror. That is my only protection from the horror about to envelop me.

As I write this, it's pitch dark outside – long after midnight. I am in a bedroom I've never slept in before, and I can't make too much noise, in case I wake up the person sleeping in the other bed.

I suppose I could go downstairs. But I'd just have people pretending to be cheerful – or looking at me so pityingly.

Yet sleep is miles away. And I have to do something. So I've decided I shall tell you my incredible story. That way, at least a little part of me will go on existing.

Firstly, though, I have an important warning for you. Once it was fine to keep your head in the sand and pretend vampires didn't exist. For until recently vampires stayed away from humans. In real life, you see, they don't even like human blood. It's far too sour for them – they actually live off animal blood instead.

But now – and please listen carefully to what I'm telling you – there is a new sect, known as *the deadly vampires*. They have discovered that however repulsive they find the taste of human blood, if drunk in large enough quantities, it can give them undreamed-of new powers – while totally draining humans of their strength and energy, of course.

They are the most dangerous vampires in the whole world, and they believe their days in the shadows are over. They want to bring back the vampire glory days.

And the first demonstration of their amazing new powers took place here in Great Walden, the village where I live, just a few months ago.

So who am I? I should have told you sooner. Sorry, but my head is all over the place tonight. I'm Tallulah. I'm thirteen years old and I'm a bit of a weirdo. Ask anyone. And I don't care. Well, who wants to be normal and ordinary? Not me. By the way, I'm also a total loner. For most of my life I've never had a single friend.

But I didn't need friends. Instead, I lived in a dream world of books and comics and films, and all about one thing: the wildest and most twisted outsiders of all – *vampires*. Before I knew they were real, I was obsessed with them. And I had an open mind about something which most humans will never even consider, namely the possibility of another world existing apart from the obvious, totally tedious one around us. Kind of ironic now, I suppose.

I'd always had the strangest feeling that there was another reality – and vampires were a massive part of it. But even I never expected the insanely dull village where I live to become a war zone.

Pitched on one side were the deadly vampires.

On the other were just three people – me, a vampire expert called Cyril, and Marcus.

Marcus is the total opposite to me. I'm hard to like. He's practically impossible to dislike. He's the kind of cheeky schoolboy who is always making you laugh from the back row of the classroom, lighting up even the most boring lesson.

Marcus will hate me telling you this next bit. But once, late at night, I heard Cyril and him having a big argument (which was very strange in itself, as Marcus hardly ever gets mad). Cyril was saying that he thought Marcus might be a half-vampire, or have relatives who were. Marcus got really angry and said he didn't even know what half-vampires were. (In case you don't, they're completely peaceful and friendly, living alongside humans but never revealing their secret identity. They don't ever drink human blood, and they are the enemy of true, evil vampires. They can also shape-change into bats, and some of them have other extra gifts.)

Later, when I asked Marcus about this, he got furious all over again and denied it once more.

But sometimes I wonder . . .

Anyway, when we battled the deadly vampires before, Marcus and I were in great danger, but it was a magic kind of danger, binding us together. We ended up defeating them and saving the world (not that the world ever knew) and I'd made my first ever friend.

Best time of my life, no question. Especially when Marcus asked me out. I never thought a boy would ever do that. Or that I'd ever want to go out with a boy. But I did, even though I said 'No' to Marcus at first. Well, it took me by surprise, him asking me out – and on the ghost train, of all places. But I thought I'd have plenty of time to reverse that decision.

Only I didn't.

Marcus's family had to move to Paris for a few months and of course he had to go with them.

And as if that wasn't bad enough, I became really ill. No doctor could tell me what was wrong, and I couldn't shake it off either. So in the end I had to go away to a special hospital, called a sanatorium, and be a human guinea pig (*'Just one more test, Tallulah'*) for weeks and weeks. Maddening beyond belief.

Especially as all the time I was wondering what the deadly vampires were planning next. We'd only won the first round, after all.

But at last the sanatorium told me they'd tried all the tests they could think of, and I was allowed to leave. They even let me out three days early – on Easter Saturday. Meanwhile, I'd also heard from Marcus that he had just arrived home from Paris. That was marvellous news, as I so wanted to see him again.

And this is where my story really begins – and ends.

# PART ONE

## *Tallulah*

# CHAPTER ONE

## *A Horrible Surprise*

When I arrived home from the sanatorium I got such a strange reaction from my family. They were actually quite pleased to see me. I kept looking behind to see if someone else had walked in with me.

You see, I'm the black sheep of the family – but you've guessed that already. Still, it's hard not to be when you've got an older brother, Martin, who is in the opinion of everyone – not least himself – a genius. And a younger sister, Glynis, who's won prizes for dancing, swimming, gymnastics, even gardening. And if they gave out awards for being adorable she'd snap up every one of them. She's managed to fool everybody – except me.

Who on earth could live up to those two?

Well, I don't even bother to try.

But that night I had to endure a family meal to celebrate my return. There was Dad booming questions at me (and not really listening to any of the answers, of course), Mum trilling, 'Aren't we having fun,' every five seconds, and me hemmed in like a prisoner between Glynis and Martin for two whole hours of my life that I'll never get back.

But finally, finally I was able to jump up from the table and say, 'I'm just going out for a bit.'

'Wherever are you going?' asked Mum at once.

'Only down the road to see Marcus,' I said, as casually as I could.

'She's going all red,' cooed Glynis in her delightful way.

'But must you go tonight?' cried Mum. 'You've been very ill, you know.'

'Yeah, bring that up as often as possible, Mum. It really cheers me up.'

'You must wrap up,' went on Mum.

'I'm not leading an expedition to Antarctica,' I muttered.

Then Dad announced I had to be home in just forty minutes from now. Hardly any time at all. But it was still going to be brilliant, especially as I hadn't even texted Marcus to say I was coming back. So what a top surprise he'd get when he saw me standing on his doorstep, three days earlier than expected.

After I rang Marcus's doorbell my heart began beating really fast, as if I'd run twenty miles to get here, not walked for about five minutes. There was silence at first. Then I heard these shuffling movements.

A shiver ran up my spine – without me knowing why.

Seconds later the door opened and there was Marcus, giving his usual goofy grin but also leaning on a walking stick. That was a shock. But I was so happy to see him that I wouldn't have cared if he'd been holding onto ten walking sticks.

Then I gave Marcus a big hug. Or rather, I started to, until I noticed my hug was a bit one-sided. Marcus was merely patting me a

11

little as if I were a stray dog who'd turned up at his door. He was also gaping at me in a totally bewildered way.

I stepped back from him. 'I wanted to surprise you, and I see I have.'

Marcus replied, 'I loved the hug. Thanks very much. But who exactly are you?'

# CHAPTER TWO

### *Memory Loss*

Marcus makes jokes the way most of us breathe in and out. He just can't stop doing it. But to pretend he didn't even know who I was? That wasn't remotely funny, especially as I'd been so looking forward to this reunion. He'd spoiled everything.

And then I had a really horrible thought. Being in a sanatorium doesn't exactly enhance your looks. That's why I'd totally avoided looking at myself lately. But I knew I was much thinner, and my skin was deathly white and all zitty. So was Marcus saying he just didn't like me any more?

'Have I changed very much?' I asked.

'No,' he began. 'Well, actually I don't know if you've changed or not. The thing is, I've been sucked back in time.'

'What!?'

'Yeah, flung back a whole six and a bit months to September the twenty-ninth – the day before my thirteenth birthday.'

This whole conversation was getting stranger and stranger.

'Marcus, what on earth are you talking about?'

He cleared his throat as if he were about to deliver a little speech. 'You see this walking stick? Well, it isn't my latest fashion accessory. Not long after I got home from Paris, I was knocked off my bike. And I went flying over the handlebars. *Not* a great way to travel.'

'Sounds painful,' I said.

'It was. The driver said something flew right into his windscreen – like a giant bird or bat, and that's why he didn't see me.'

'A bat,' I echoed. I didn't like the sound of that at all.

'Well, that's what he claimed. Anyway, I've bumped my head so badly it's shaken out

14

everything that's happened to me since my thirteenth birthday. So I can't remember that birthday or Christmas, or anything I did at school this term, or last term after September the twenty-ninth. And Mum insists I use this stick in case anything *else* happens, even though I can walk perfectly OK.'

'You're saying you've lost your memory – or six months of it.'

'Exactly, and if you see those six months anywhere about – I'd like them back.' He grinned a bit awkwardly. 'Actually, this doctor who's been looking after me, Dr Jasper, says memory blackouts aren't as unusual as you might think. But the really annoying thing is, people can't just fill me in on what I've got up to in my missing months. Apparently it's much better if I let my memory repair itself. And soon I'll remember everything again.'

'How soon?'

'Dr Jasper said normal service should be resumed any day now. Bit of a shock for you hearing all this.'

'Yeah,' I agreed. 'Still, even worse one for you.'

'Just a temporary blip, honestly,' he said

firmly. 'Anyway, look, come in . . . er, sorry, what's your name?'

To be telling Marcus – *Marcus* – my name was beyond odd. I tried to make a little joke of it all. 'Me Tallulah.'

'Cool name. Well, look, Tallulah, I'll crack open the Tic-tacs and maybe if we talk for a bit – well, who knows what I'll start remembering.'

I sat down in Marcus's kitchen while he made me a cup of coffee. He said, 'If it's any consolation, another girl came round here yesterday who I'd never seen in my life before either. Only I had. I know her very well, apparently.'

'Was it Gracie?'

'Yeah, do you know her?'

'A bit, yeah.'

Gracie didn't go to our school. Her mum and dad were friends with Marcus's parents, and that's how she and Marcus knew each other.

'She'd even bought me a little present for when I got back from Paris. A cute little dog. Not a real one, of course – just a china one like an ornament. Still, its eyes actually light up at night.'

So Gracie was buying him presents. I couldn't help feeling a stab of jealousy.

Then I said, 'Actually, we knew each other before your memory blackout on September the twenty-ninth. I was a new girl at your school. I'd only been there for a few weeks.'

Marcus whirled round. 'Of course.'

'You remember me,' I said eagerly.

'I remember you joining our school. I just didn't make the connection before, because today you smiled at me and seemed all sane and nice – while at school . . .' He hesitated.

'I was insane and horrible.'

'No, you terrified me, though.'

'I didn't.'

'You totally did – you had rows with just about everyone, didn't you?'

I grinned faintly.

'Even some of the teachers were shaking.'

'You're exaggerating now.'

'I'm not, and that's why I never spoke to you. I thought, *She'll eat me alive*. But now we're actually good friends?'

'Don't sound so amazed.'

'I'm not.'

'Come on, you are,' I said.

'OK, I am.' He laughed awkwardly. 'But in a totally good way. So we hang out a lot?' He just couldn't take the shock out of his voice.

'Oh yeah, mainly in the evenings.'

His eyebrows shot up. 'Mainly in the evenings? I've got a lot to remember.'

'You certainly have,' I agreed. Like how we'd fought vampires together, I thought. That's really when we got together and became friends, close friends.

But without any of these memories, what was I to Marcus? Just a stroppy, scary new girl. I so hated only being that.

Then his parents returned. They'd obviously been out shopping. But when they heard us talking they flung down all their bags and practically stampeded into the kitchen. Marcus's parents have never been my biggest fans, but today they seemed positively alarmed by my presence.

Marcus's mum was stuttering, 'Oh, T-Tallulah, we thought you were still away.'

'She is,' grinned Marcus. 'This is just a hologram. Very life-like, isn't it?'

'I got back three days early,' I said.

'And she rushed round to see me,' said

18

Marcus. 'Only I had to say sorry but this is my week for not remembering people. By the way, why didn't you ever mention Tallulah to me? You could have told me something about her.'

'Well, we knew she was in hospital,' began his dad.

'A sanatorium actually,' I corrected.

Marcus whirled round. 'I thought you'd been away on holiday. Why on earth have you been in a san— however you say it?' He sounded concerned.

'Too boring to tell you right now,' I said.

'We also didn't mention Tallulah,' said Marcus's mum, 'because of what Dr Jasper said.' She was still talking to Marcus while peering intently at me. 'We mustn't do anything to prompt your memory, however tempting that might be. In fact, that could be positively harmful.'

'So right now,' said Marcus, 'I'm for ever twelve years and three hundred and sixty-four days old. Hey, I've just had a horrible thought. I won't have to re-learn everything I've done at school since September, will I?'

'Remember, it's the Easter holidays. It's

nearly two weeks until the new term,' said his dad. 'Your memory will be back long before then.'

'Of course it will. This is just a little hiccup,' agreed his mum.

Then *my* mum rang up, saying I was only supposed to be out for forty minutes and she was worried about me getting super-tired. Marcus's parents leaped on this and practically marched me to the door.

Marcus saw me off. 'Sorry for being so massively forgetful today. The very second I start remembering I'll give you a ring.' His words were warm and friendly, but then he shot me such a puzzled look from his very bright blue eyes. He just couldn't work out where I fitted into his life.

I suppose I must be a bit of a shock for him. For anyone.

Rain was pattering down and Marcus's mum ran after me with an umbrella. 'We can't have you getting soaked through,' she said, 'not after you've just left the sanatorium.'

'Oh, thanks.'

'You must look after yourself, dear. You've been so ill.' Marcus's mum lowered her voice.

'We're not telling anyone else about Marcus's touch of amnesia. Well, it will be all sorted out very soon.'

'When exactly?' I asked.

'It's really best not to rush these things, dear.' She was looking right at me now. 'He just needs lots of rest, and peace and quiet. No hurry at all to return the umbrella,' she added, which sounded to me very like, 'No hurry for you to come back either.'

At home Mum and Dad met me at the door.

'Sorry to break up your reunion,' said Dad in that mock-hearty voice he puts on when he's not telling me off or sighing at me in door-ways, 'but you're under a curfew, young lady.'

'And the doctor did say you've got to be very careful not to become over-tired,' chipped in Mum.

'It's OK,' I said. 'And I am very tired. Night.'

Shocked by my meek tone, Mum and Dad could only stare at me. 'How is Marcus?' called Mum after me.

'Full of surprises,' I murmured. I just wanted to be on my own and try to make sense of what had happened tonight.

But then Glynis came skipping into my bedroom – she skips everywhere. 'Did you have a lovely time with Marcus, then?' she asked, all giddy with excitement.

I didn't even bother to answer her. She, with her fake adorable act, was the very last person I wanted to talk to now. 'I'm dead tired. Bye.'

But Glynis went on, 'Some of my friends say Marcus is quite cute. Did you kiss him? I bet you did. You can tell me, as I know all about boys.'

'Night, Glynis,' I muttered.

But she still didn't take the hint. Instead she came and sat right next to me on the bed, shoving an arm round my shoulder. 'Why don't you ask me what prizes I've won while you've been away?'

'Because you'll probably tell me.' Then I added gravely, 'Actually, Glynis, you'd better not get too close to me.'

'Why not?'

'Do you see all the zits on my face?'

'No one could miss them.'

'Well, the thing is, they could fall off at

any moment. In fact, I think one might have just landed on you now.'

'Oh, yuk, yuk, where?' squealed Glynis, jumping to her feet. Then she saw me smiling and cried, 'I think you are the weirdest, most disgusting sister ever.'

'That's what I live for.'

Before flouncing off, Glynis left me with a final thought. 'I bet Marcus will soon get himself a much prettier girlfriend than you!'

# CHAPTER THREE

## *The Call of the Vampire*

Easter Sunday came and went – Marcus didn't ring. But I spent hours and hours wondering: had he started remembering? And had he started remembering *me* yet?

And every so often a feeling of uneasiness would steal over me.

Marcus's accident – and memory loss – had been caused by a large bird or bat flying into that driver's window.

A bat.

I kept coming back to that. Was that just an odd coincidence?

I so wanted to help Marcus and do something, but instead I was stuck in this limbo. But then, on Easter Monday, over yet another family meal, came a piece of news which was to prove extremely important.

We'd gone out to a restaurant this time, with the slowest service known to humanity, when my brother suddenly turned to me and said, 'A new shop opened last week which I'm sure you'll be interested in.'

I doubted this very much as I hate all shopping.

'It's called Mad About Monsters,' he added.

I was interested in that all right.

'It's quite small and right at the end of all the new shops in Dover Street. And the window's full of pictures of monsters. In fact, it's a bit like looking at your bedroom wall.'

All my family had a little chortle here.

'Of course, I didn't have time to go in myself,' Martin went on.

No, he'd leave that to his mad sister. But I'd certainly be paying Mad About Monsters a visit. Of all the places to open such a specialist shop, Great Walden seemed a most unlikely choice, unless . . .

My mind was racing now. When the deadly vampires had arrived here before, they'd come with the fair, and pretended to work on some of the stalls and rides. Was this another way for them to return? Was that shop merely a cover for vampire activities?

And Marcus losing his memory in the very same week Mad About Monsters opened. Was that just another coincidence?

First thing next morning I paid the shop a visit. There it was with 'Just Opened' spread right across the window and a truly dazzling display of posters of all sorts of monsters.

When I opened the door a loud howl broke out. I'd so love to have a similar sound effect fixed to my bedroom door. It really made me feel at home.

The shop itself might have been very small but it was just crammed with stuff – and all of it fascinating. The really expensive models were in glass cases at astronomical prices. But there were much cheaper little monsters and horror DVDs and books and eye-catching posters . . . this was, without doubt, the most exciting shop I'd ever been in.

Then I heard a voice say, 'Our first customer of the day, how splendid.' A small, middle-aged man with a ginger beard was weaving his way over to me. There was nothing unusual about him, except for a large black eye patch over his right eye.

He beamed at me, pink-faced and welcoming. But I wasn't fooled. Once I'd met such a charming, sweet old lady called Mrs Lenchester, who had turned out to be a truly deadly vampire.

Could he be another one?

'Herbert Cheshire at your service. Welcome to my little kingdom,' he said, rolling every word round his tongue like an actor out of an ancient black and white film. 'Maybe we are tiny but we're teeming with terror – *King Kong*, *The Creature from the Black Lagoon*, *Godzilla*, *Jaws*, *The Terror from Beyond Space*, winged serpents, werewolves, they're all here, even *The Invisible Man*.'

I smiled politely at his little joke.

'But I think' – he paused and seemed to be studying me for a moment – 'in fact, I'm certain that it's one of the classics you have come to see. Vampires.'

I started with surprise. 'But how on earth did you know that?'

'Matching up people with monsters is my job,' he said. 'No, it isn't – it's my *calling*. Now kindly follow me.' And he led the way to the vampire section.

It was impossible to miss actually, as a large black cloak hovered over us there. It stirred slightly and had what looked like the remains of blood, though was probably really tomato sauce, round its edges.

Herbert Cheshire saw me admiring the cape and said, 'I'm afraid that isn't for sale.'

'Is it yours?'

For a moment he seemed taken aback by my question, but then he said smoothly, 'Yes, it is, actually. I'm an ardent collector myself. Well, I will leave you to browse. I'm sure you will find much of interest here.'

I did, and for a while I was so riveted, so totally transfixed by the magnificent collection of vampire books (both new and second-hand), DVDs and masks, I forgot everything else. But then I looked up at the cape again. The fact that it belonged to the shop's owner could well be a clue to his true nature. But would he be quite so obvious about it? Still, vampires can be quite arrogant, practically daring you to challenge them.

From time to time the owner looked over at me and waved genially. There was still no one else in the shop. Then finally he bounded over. 'May I enquire how you are getting on?'

'Just finished, and I've already picked out too much.'

'Ah, there's nothing like a good scare for helping us forget our troubles, is there?' he said. 'Once inside my snug and cosy shop you can shut out the tedium and dreariness of the dark world outside. So drop in any time.'

'Thanks, I will. Er . . . do you work here alone?'

'No, I have an assistant down below.' He pointed at the steps leading downstairs. 'Most of our business is done via the internet. We have customers from all over the world, you know. But we needed a base, and the rent on our last place rocketed, so we moved here, which is, happily, eminently affordable. Now, shall I take your purchases, including that splendid vampire mask?' He bobbed over to a very old-fashioned cash till.

'Go on then, tell me the worst,' I said.

'Oh, I'm sure we can manage a small discount for our regular customers, and I know you're going to be one of our regulars.' He actually gave me a large discount, and while I was paying I noticed that there was a box containing china models of cute little Jack Russell dogs by the till. I remembered Marcus telling me about the toy dog Gracie had bought for him, and wondered if this was where she had got it. But what were they doing in a shop devoted to monsters?

Herbert Cheshire looked across at me, and as if reading my thoughts said, 'Those charming creatures are my assistant's idea. Andy's quite taken with them, though I suspect it's all a joke on me really. You see, I have a faithful little Jack Russell called Pluto, but one day Pluto jumped up to lick my face and accidentally removed an eye instead.'

'That's awful!'

'It was for both of us. Poor Pluto was mortified, especially as he'd accidentally swallowed my eye. But the doctor said later that even if I'd brought it in they wouldn't have been able to sew it back into its socket. Still, I'm delighted to say, Pluto and I remain the closest of companions. And I can manage with one eye quite satisfactorily.'

Before I could ask Herbert Cheshire anything else, the werewolf howl announced new customers – a whole family this time – so Herbert handed me my purchases and then started going through his 'Welcome to my little kingdom' patter with them. But as I was leaving he called after me, 'We look forward to welcoming you again soon.'

For the rest of the day I kept thinking about Mad About Monsters and its eye patch-wearing owner. I even dreamed about him that night, about the moment when Pluto realized what he'd done to his owner. He howled in misery, the poor dog, a truly heart-rending sound.

Then I shot awake and I could still hear Pluto, or so I thought at first. It was definitely a howling noise. But it wasn't the cry of a dog or any animal, I was certain of that. I recognized this blood-chilling sound. It belonged to a supernatural creature – *a vampire*.

I switched on my light. Still the howling noise went on. Then I opened my bedroom door. Someone else in my family must surely have heard it too. I wanted to share this creepy sound with someone – anyone. I peered into each of the family bedrooms. But everyone seemed to be lost in a really deep sleep. Everyone except me. So now what should I do? Go and wake up one of my family. But what would they do? And maybe they wouldn't even hear it. Then another thought crept into my head.

Maybe it was just me who could pick up that gruesome sound.

Immediately something leaped and tingled inside me.

I was scared all right, but I also felt more alive than I had in weeks and weeks.

So after hastily getting dressed I packed a torch (checking the batteries first), some plasters, just in case I got attacked, and to make sure that didn't happen I crammed both my pockets full of garlic (I always keep a good supply in my bedroom).

Next I had to leave the house without anyone realizing. This can be quite tricky, but

I've learned not to make any more sound than a passing ghost. So even if you had supersonic hearing I don't think you'd have heard me creep downstairs and ever so carefully open the front door.

Then I stepped outside.

# CHAPTER FOUR

## *The Figure in Black*

The street lights bathed everything in an orange glow and sent my shadow stretching out behind me, making me seem enormously tall and ready to face – well, what exactly?

The very moment I stepped outside the vampire cry had stopped. Was that a bit suspicious? Was I walking straight into a trap? But everything around me was deathly still save for the trees stirring lightly in the breeze. No one seemed to be about.

And then something happened which made me jump into the air with shock.

The street lights all went out together.

It happened so suddenly it felt as if some supernatural creature must have been involved, plunging everything into total darkness. I peered around anxiously until I remembered reading in the local paper about the council switching off all the lights in the middle of the night to save money. That was all that had just happened – nothing spooky about it.

Only it was so dark now it was hard to see where I was going. I was just reaching for my torch when my whole body went rigid with terror. One of the shadows right ahead of me had started to move. No one had been there a few seconds ago – I was absolutely certain of that. But now there was certainly someone, a figure that seemed to have just risen out of the darkness. Then the figure glanced around. I immediately shrank back and put my torch away. It turned away again and started moving so fast it was practically running.

Where was it going? Of course I had to follow it – even though the way it had just appeared out of the air made me certain that I was trailing a vampire.

I clutched my garlic tightly. My hands were shaking, but after months of rusting away in that sanatorium I was so pleased to be back doing what I did best – tracking down vampires. I was sure this was a deadly vampire as well – one of the most dangerous vampires. And I was so close to it. Could my night get any better?

Well, of course it could – if Marcus had been here with me. Every second there was this giant hole beside me. Still, I thought, when Marcus gets his memory back, what a story I'll have to tell him. And he'll be so impressed by my bravery, roaming about at night all on my own. I was quite impressed with it myself.

Once the dark figure stopped and twisted round sharply. Had it heard me? But then it set off again, only to stop shortly afterwards – right outside Marcus's house.

That was a shock. But in another way it wasn't, if you know what I mean.

I strained to see what it was doing. It didn't seem to be doing anything at all at first. It was just standing there and staring up at Marcus's bedroom window. It might have been a sentry on duty. And for what felt like ages and ages it went on not doing anything.

I edged closer. I could see the figure more clearly now. It was a boy, not much older than me, and he was dressed entirely in black. But who was he? And why was he lurking outside Marcus's house? Could he really be a vampire? I felt so sure he was.

Did he have anything to do with Mad About Monsters? The idea just popped into my head. Hadn't Herbert Cheshire talked about his young assistant, Andy? Could this be Andy? Maybe he and Herbert Cheshire were both deadly vampires.

All at once the boy started to move, or rather his hands did. They were circling about and then snatching forward, as if he were trying to grab an invisible ball out of the air.

He was muttering something too. It was incredibly faint though, so I couldn't catch any of the words. But it was the way he spoke which chilled me. He seemed to be chanting something over and over, as if he were casting a spell – on Marcus.

A spell which would make certain Marcus's

memory didn't return? Was that what he was doing? I was sure it was. It all made sense.

The deadly vampires had caused the accident which resulted in Marcus banging his head and forgetting everything about his time as a vampire hunter. And now they were making sure Marcus's memory stayed shot to pieces and couldn't interfere with whatever fresh horror they were planning.

I was just a little bit hurt that the deadly vampires hadn't bothered to stop me remembering them too. Did they think I was so unimportant? Still, it was extremely lucky that they had so badly underestimated me.

And if I stopped this deadly vampire from finishing the spell he was casting on Marcus, would his memory come back? It was certainly worth finding out.

Grabbing the garlic from both pockets and turning my hands into fists I charged forward. 'Hey, stop doing that!' I shouted. 'Leave him alone.' I was so fired up I was ready to fight that vampire. I really was.

But in a flash he just melted away into the shadows. I was almost disappointed he hadn't even tried to take me on. And why did he leave so quickly? Was it because of all the garlic I was clutching?

And, most important, had I been in time to save Marcus's memory being messed with even further? So many questions were dashing through my head as I stood there, shaking with horror and shock and anger at what I'd seen tonight.

I wanted to tear into Marcus's house and tell him what had just happened. Surely he had a right to know. But all I'd really seen was a boy waving his hands about and whispering outside his house.

I had no proof at all that he was a vampire, other than the way he'd appeared and disappeared.

Marcus's parents would just say I'd imagined the whole thing. And before I knew what was happening they'd have rung up my mum and dad, who'd be absolutely furious that I was roaming about in the middle of the night. They'd probably ground me for the next six months as well.

So I didn't burst into Marcus's house. Instead, I walked home, just thinking, thinking,

thinking. Of course, it was the purest luck I'd discovered the vampire tonight.

No, it wasn't.

I stopped walking.

It was the vampire cry I'd heard that had sent me outside. Had someone woken me up on purpose? But that didn't make any sense at all. Why would the vampires *want* me to discover what they were up to?

I crept up the stairs into my bedroom. I didn't even try to sleep. How could I?

I'd been forbidden by Marcus's parents to actually tell him anything about the last months. And I did agree that it would be better if his memory came back naturally. But I needed to really speed things up.

Then it hit me. Mad About Monsters. Of course! Of course! I'd take Marcus there, let him roam around that epic shop, and before long it would be prompting all sorts of memories without me needing to say a word.

I couldn't wait to ring Marcus, but actually he called me first, early next morning.

'Can you come over to my house right away?' he said.

'Why?'

'I'll tell you when you get here – but hurry.'

And with that he put the phone down.

Why can

[I] [t]ell you when you get here?' but

Marky ——

She went before I put the phone down.

# CHAPTER FIVE

## *The Vampire Returns*

I zoomed round to Marcus's house.

He'd started remembering, hadn't he? That's why he wanted to see me urgently.

Then I thought of something else – did Marcus's memory returning (and I'd convinced myself that this was what had happened) mean that I'd stopped the deadly vampire casting a spell last night? I really must have. I'd scared away a deadly vampire. Me!

There was no need for me to take him to Mad About Monsters after all. Marcus's memory was back!

I'd worked everything out in my head

before I even saw Marcus. No wonder I was so excited.

There he was, waiting on the doorstep for me. And the second I arrived he started talking out of the side of his mouth, doing quite a clever impersonation of actors in old gangster films.

'Hey, I knew you wouldn't let me down – now, can you run?'

'On a good day.'

'And I can limp – what a team we'll make. Come on, then.'

'But where are we going?'

'Anywhere you like,' he said as he started off down his drive, 'provided it takes me right away from my parents. Every second now they ask me if I'm feeling relaxed. And nothing is less relaxing than being constantly asked if you're relaxed. In fact, I'm thinking of applying to stay in a high-security prison, just for a bit of privacy.' He gave his familiar wide grin. 'So cheers for rescuing me.'

'Is that what I've done?' We were moving at quite a pace down his road now.

'Yeah, my mum had to drive Dad somewhere as his car's all clapped out. So I saw my chance to break out and see you.'

I stared at him expectantly. But he wasn't adding what I was sure he was going to tell me. So I said it for him. 'Your memory's come back, hasn't it?'

'No, not a sausage.'

I was too stunned to be disappointed at first. I was so absolutely convinced that was why he'd called me. 'You still don't remember anything?' I said.

'Well, the odd flash of memory, yeah, but nothing concrete. A bit frustrating, really. That's why I thought if I hung out with you, well, that might stop me being imprisoned for ever in September the twenty-ninth of last year – if that is OK, Tallulah.' He said my name so shyly it was kind of cute.

'Of course it's OK.'

'So where shall we go?'

It was time to activate my original plan. 'Well, we could drop in on a new shop called Mad About Monsters.'

'That sounds freaky,' said Marcus.

'I think you'll enjoy it,' I said, setting off.

'Hey, you're a fast walker,' he said.

I just wanted to get there and for Marcus to start remembering. And I was absolutely certain this was the place to do it. Mr Herbert Cheshire and his not-yet-seen assistant, Andy, were my top suspects for deadly vampires, of course. It would be kind of ironic if their shop was the trigger for Marcus's memory returning.

I walked into that shop tense with expect-ation – and hope.

Herbert Cheshire steamed over to us, a large mug of tea in his hand. 'Ah now, I see an old friend,' he said to me. 'And you've brought a chum with you – how perfectly splendid. May I assist you, or would you prefer a good old browse?'

'We'll browse, thanks,' I said.

'Browse to your heart's content,' said Mr Cheshire, and then sped off to greet some other new customers.

'He's as wacky as this shop,' grinned Marcus. '*You've brought a chum with you,*' he repeated, shaking his head disbelievingly. 'And why's he dressed like a geriatric pirate?'

'He's not,' I began. 'I'll tell you later.' But I actually never did explain to Marcus how

Herbert Cheshire lost his eye – and it's too late now.

Three other people were in the shop that day: two guys in trench coats and big Doc Marten boots, and a girl dressed completely in black. All three were unsmiling and miserable-looking.

'Hey,' said Marcus to me, nodding over at them, 'I can see why you feel really at home here.'

I suppose I did dress a bit like them. But it wasn't exactly a flattering comment.

'So what shall we look at first?' he continued.

'I'll take you on a tour,' I said. I'd only been here once myself, but already this shop felt like a second home to me. I decided to lead up to the vampires, so we went to the werewolf section first, then the *Jaws* exhibition, after which I couldn't wait any longer and we moved off to see the vampires.

'What about this, then?' I said, peering up at the vampire cloak.

But Marcus was already looking at a model of a vampire and grinning. 'Pointy teeth, not a good look,' he went on. 'I never got why people go all crazy about vampires. I mean, drinking blood is just so anti-social, isn't it? And all the vampires I've seen on films whine on endlessly. I want to say them, "Get over yourself." ' Then he added, 'Shall we go for a coffee in a minute?'

'You don't want to stay here?' I was crushed, devastated.

'Not unless you do. Vampires just aren't my thing.'

'Yes they are.'

'What did you say?' he asked.

'You and I, we're . . .'

He moved closer. 'We're what?'

And I nearly said 'vampire hunters'. The words were right there in my mouth. I so wanted to blurt them out. But I knew if I did I'd be forcing things and could maybe prevent Marcus's memory returning naturally.

So instead I just said in this weird, muffled voice, 'We'll leave now.'

'No, look, if you want to stay . . .'

'No, no, you want to go, so that's what we'll do.' I was sounding all huffy now but I couldn't help it – I'd been certain that being here surrounded by vampires would prompt so many memories. But instead we'd ended up further apart than ever.

We were at the door of the shop when Marcus swerved away from me. 'Now what are *you* doing here?' he said. 'All these ghosts and ghoulies will eat you for breakfast.' He'd spotted the cute little dogs at the cash till. 'These are just like the one Gracie bought for me. Mine's better, though – its eyes are black, not brown, and they glow in the dark. Must be a special one.'

Suddenly Herbert Cheshire rose up from behind the counter where he must have been sorting out some stuff extremely quietly. 'All feedback on the dogs to my assistant, Andy,' he said.

'Is Andy here?' I asked.

'Frustratingly, no,' said Herbert. 'Andy is an extraordinarily bad timekeeper. Too many late nights, if you ask me.'

I wouldn't be a bit surprised, I thought.

'But you're not leaving already?' asked Herbert.

'I'm afraid so. My friend's just not inter-ested in any of this,' I said bitterly.

'Cheers for that,' murmured Marcus. But

outside the shop he was grinning at me again. 'Sorry.'

'What for?'

'I've insulted you, haven't I?'

'No.'

'Yes I have, because you really, really like horror. In fact, I'd say you're addicted to it. I'm sorry for not being a fellow believer. But tonight I'll watch three Dracula films while eating garlic to make up for it. How about that?' He was teasing me, but I was still too knotted up with disappointment to respond.

So I just grunted something.

Marcus went on. 'Looking at you, I'd also say you're a bit of a tomboy.'

Now if there's one thing I loathe and despise, it's being called a tomboy. It's beyond patronizing for a start, and totally untrue. So I immediately burst out, 'Actually I've never wanted to be a boy. I just don't like dressing up or makeup and I love horror. But I'm still a girl – I'm just a different *kind* of girl, that's all.'

Marcus didn't say one word in reply, only nodded very slightly, but I could actually feel him shrinking away from me. Instantly I longed to take my words back. Marcus didn't know me at all right now so he was bound to make mistakes. Why on earth couldn't I make allowances for him? What was the matter with me today?

No wonder he didn't say anything else to me as we walked down the street. I couldn't think of anything to say either. So the silence just grew until someone selling flowers shuffled towards us. A guy with a cloth cap which was hiding most of his face came right up to Marcus. 'Buy some flowers for the young lady.'

'Yeah, sure,' said Marcus at once.

'You don't have to,' I began.

'Look on it as a peace offering for daring to call you a tomboy and for the many other things I got wrong today,' said Marcus. 'Hey, you're not allergic to flowers, are you? They don't give you hay fever or mumps or rashes . . . ?'

'Strangely enough, they don't.'

'Wow, what a result.' And no – I didn't miss the edge of sarcasm in Marcus's voice either. Someone buying you flowers might sound romantic. But this didn't feel the least like that. I knew Marcus was doing it more as a kind of joke really. 'So do you want to choose what you'd like?' he asked. 'There are some manky-looking daffs and some not so manky-looking daffs.'

He was being so rude, but the flower-seller didn't seem to mind. In fact, he started laughing. 'We also have manky-looking tulips,' he said.

'Would you like some tulips?' Marcus asked me.

I started to answer but then I caught sight of the flower-seller's eyes.

Big, staring eyes which I'd seen before.

They belonged to the vampire from outside Marcus's house last night.

# CHAPTER SIX

## *A Cry for Help*

I gazed at the flower-seller again. There was no mistake. But what on earth was a vampire doing here, making himself known to Marcus? What was he up to?

'So are you going with the tulips?' asked Marcus a bit impatiently. 'You seem dazzled by the lack of choice.'

But the shock had caused my throat to go into spasm and so I was unable to speak. Finally I managed to move my head very slowly. Marcus shot me a curious glance. Then he started peering into his wallet saying, 'It's awfully dark in there.'

The flower-seller was still laughing, but all the time he kept looking at Marcus. In fact, his eyes seemed glued to Marcus. He totally ignored me.

'I've never seen you selling flowers here before,' Marcus said to him.

'It's a new pitch for me,' he said, handing Marcus his change and wrapping up the tulips. 'And you are my first sale.'

'Well, what about that?' grinned Marcus. 'So you've started with the best.'

At last I found my voice. 'I know you, don't I?' I asked the flower-seller suddenly.

'I don't think so,' he replied. 'I'm sure I would have remembered.' His voice had the trace of a French accent. He gave me a little bow as he handed Marcus the flowers, then he sped away.

Marcus gave them to me with something of a flourish. Then he looked at me anxiously. 'Hey, are you all right, Tallulah? You're shaking.'

'Yeah, I'm fine.'

'That flower-seller. You thought you knew him.'

'Er, yeah,' I said vaguely. My face still felt as if it were on fire.

'So what's his name?'

'I don't know.'

'He doesn't go to our school, does he?'

'No.'

'So how do you know him?'

I so wanted to reply, *Because I saw him outside your house last night, trying to put a spell on you, and he is, in fact, a deadly vampire.* But of course I wasn't able to say any of this so I just snapped, 'Look, what is this, an interrogation? Let's just forget him.'

'OK, he's forgotten.' Marcus sounded puzzled and hurt and I knew exactly what he was thinking: *This girl's a total weirdo, and a real handful. How did I ever get hooked up with her?*

And then a familiar voice called out, 'So there you are,' and hurtling towards us came Gracie. I'm sure I heard Marcus heave a sigh of relief. Certainly the atmosphere lightened instantly. She's a really pretty girl with long, dark hair and wide, shining green eyes, and yes, incredibly nice. And I so wished she wasn't here now. She just seemed to magnify my prickliness.

'Oh hi, Tallulah,' she cried. 'Did Marcus buy you those tulips to welcome you home?'

'Sort of,' I muttered.

'He never buys me flowers,' she laughed. Then she gave me a hug. But she couldn't have been as pleased to see me as she was letting on. We'd only met a couple of times. She was Marcus's friend, not mine. 'Are you feeling better now?' she asked, sounding all concerned.

'Oh yeah,' I said vaguely.

Gracie turned to Marcus. 'I've been round your house. Your mum's in a total flap.'

'Just for a change,' said Marcus.

'She said you went off without even telling her where you were going. *And* you left your stick behind too.' She giggled. 'So I thought I'd walk into town and look around, see if I could find you.'

'Not all true,' said Marcus. 'I wrote her a marvellous note which I left . . .' He thought for a moment, and then he pulled it out. 'Right here in my pocket. Still, she can read it later.' They grinned at each other.

Then Gracie asked him, 'So do you like my hair?'

'Yeah, great – your best hair ever. What have you done?'

'What have I done!' she exclaimed mock-indignantly. 'I was over an hour at the hairdresser's yesterday.'

'And it was worth it. I love hilarious hair.'

She started to hit him then while they were both laughing. He didn't remember Gracie either. But you'd never have guessed it. Somehow they still fitted. How on earth had she managed that?

Gracie rattled on for ages about how she'd landed this part in a play her school was putting on. She was all excited, even though it was only a small role.

'But you should have the lead,' declared Marcus. He hardly knew her, yet he was showering her with compliments.

Gracie's smile only faltered once. That was when Marcus said to her, 'Hey, I know where you got me that toy dog. It was at that new shop, Mad About Monsters. I didn't know you were into ghoulish stuff.'

A flash of embarrassment – even shame – crossed Gracie's face then. And I thought how silly people can be. What on earth was wrong with girls dropping into Mad About Monsters?

She quickly changed the subject by suggesting we all have a coffee. She and Marcus started debating where we should all go. And I suddenly felt lonelier than I ever had before.

That's why I looked at my watch and said, 'Hey, is that the time? I was supposed to be back home ages ago . . . to do . . . something so boring I've even forgotten what it is. Still, I'd better go.'

I wouldn't win any acting awards for that. But neither would Marcus for the way he said to me, as I was going, 'I had a really good time.'

'Me too,' I lied.

Walking home, part of my mind was trying to figure out just why the vampire had turned up like that. The other part went with Marcus and Gracie to the coffee shop. With me out of the way they could really relax and have fun together. I bet they never stopped laughing and she could go on some more about that boring play she was in. I was getting so mad picturing them together that I sort of forgot I was holding those stupid tulips, until Mum and Glynis spotted me from the kitchen window.

'Did Marcus give you those?' demanded Glynis, leaping out at me. 'I bet he did.'

'I can't remember the last time anyone bought me flowers,' cooed Mum. 'What a lovely gesture. I'll find a nice vase for them.'

'No, don't bother,' I muttered.

'It's no bother at all,' said Mum. They fussed about and Mum seemed to think this was such a big moment in my life – a boy buying me flowers. I suppose it might have been if it had meant anything, but I knew it didn't.

And in my bedroom, those tulips in their posh vase just sat sneering at me. In fact, they had such a bad attitude I had to dump them all in the bin.

Then I told myself to forget everything except that vampire. I'd been too shocked to react when the vampire exploded into my day. But now I had so many questions for him. And he wouldn't scare me again.

But was he still selling his flowers in town? It was quite possible he was. He was obviously using that as a cover to observe Marcus. He might even try and contact Marcus again. But just what was he up to? It was time to find out.

Of course, I really didn't want to bump into Marcus and Gracie again, but I figured they'd be in the café for some time yet. And if I did come across them I'd just have to pretend I was doing some errands for my mum . . .

I went back into town and searched around the shopping area where we'd seen him before. No sign of the vampire anywhere. Then I wondered if he'd dropped into Mad About Monsters. I wondered again if he might even be this highly elusive shop assistant, Andy. Then I realized that was a bit unlikely, actually – Andy could hardly be working in Mad About Monsters *and* selling flowers just outside. But one thing I was certain about: the key to the whole mystery was there in that shop.

I didn't go inside at first. I just stood peering through the window. I could see Herbert Cheshire wandering about, and a few customers, but no one else.

Then a voice behind me, with the hint of

a French accent, said, 'Don't turn round.'

The vampire had moved so soundlessly I'd never heard him. He was standing right next to me now. I glanced at him, my heart beating fast, but I just said, 'Sold all your flowers then?'

He ignored this. 'Just keep looking at the window as if nothing has happened.'

'Nothing has happened.'

'Not yet. I need your help, Tallulah.'

'Who are you?' I asked. 'And how come you know my name?' I was sure Marcus hadn't used it when he bought me the tulips.

He hesitated. 'I am Jean-Paul, and just like you I want to help Marcus.'

'So you're not a vampire?'

'It is my mission to stop them. You can help me – and Marcus.' He looked around. 'But it is too dangerous to talk here any more.'

'Dangerous?' I repeated incredulously.

'The vampires are all over this place. They're probably watching us now. But later on, say about three o'clock this afternoon, at the wood nearby—'

'Brent Wood,' I interrupted.

'Yes, is there some place . . . ?'

'A little way into the wood there's a big holly bush.'

'I'll find it and I can tell you more then. No more questions now.' And with that he was gone.

When he said he wanted to stop the vampires, he'd sounded very convincing. Of course, he could just be a good actor and the whole thing might be a massive trap. Marcus is out of action, after all. Now they might want to make sure I am as well.

But up close, he didn't *seem* like a vampire.

Still, I knew I'd better be careful. So before I set off in the afternoon, I made sure I was fully armed with garlic.

I reached Brent Wood some time before three o'clock. No wind breathed here and hardly any of the afternoon sunshine broke through either. No wonder that, even in the daytime – which didn't really feel like daytime here – the stillness pressed in on you. It was actually a relief to spot two people out walking their dogs. Something normal. Both nodded and said hello to me.

But no sign of Jean-Paul.

I even whispered his name in case he was hiding somewhere. But only silence answered me.

And he never turned up.

I was so frustrated and disappointed. What could have happened to him? And would he be outside Marcus's house again tonight?

I strongly suspected he would.

Well, I'd be there too, and then I'd ask him all the questions I'd intended to ask him at three o'clock.

Later, as night pressed against the windows, I crept down the stairs.

As I was opening the front door I thought I heard a sound upstairs. I froze. It would just be awful if my dad came pounding down the stairs now. His face would fall off with shock if he spotted me trying to sneak outside. But everything was still again. So I eased open the front door and then I was off.

Once again the street lights were suddenly extinguished, just as if someone had blown them all out. But they only made me jump a little this time. And the stars were sharp and clear tonight. I practically ran to Marcus's house, fully expecting to see that vampire or whatever he was hovering outside again.

Only he wasn't there.

I was almost disappointed. Maybe he would turn up later. Well, I'd wait – I'd wait all night if necessary. I was determined.

And then the darkness was shaken by an anguished cry, followed by pounding footsteps and loud, wheezing gasps. A figure lunged towards me.

It was Jean-Paul.

# CHAPTER SEVEN

## *Return of an Enemy?*

He clutched at me. He could hardly stand up.
I shone my torch. Sweat was pouring down
his face and neck. He looked wild-eyed, terrified. And he was hanging onto me so hard
I was worried he was going to pull us both
over.

'You've been attacked – by vampires . . . !'
I said.

But he couldn't speak. He was still struggling to breathe. As gently as I could I guided
and supported him to the nearest wall. He sat
there, shaking all over. It took a while for him
to be able to breathe normally again.

Then I said, 'I've got some plasters and stuff.' I carefully wiped his face, which was streaked with blood, and put a plaster over a particularly deep scratch. 'Do you want some water?' I asked.

'Oh, yes, yes please,' he gasped.

I dug into my pocket and produced the little bottle of water I always carry with me at night. He grabbed the bottle and was so eager to drink it he spilled some down his face.

Then he looked up at me. 'I have drunk it all, I'm sorry.'

'Not a problem. I've got some chocolate as well. Would you like some of that?'

'Oh yes.' He wolfed that down too, and then he smiled at me. 'Tonight you are my guardian angel.'

'Well, no one's ever called me that before.' I laughed, a bit flattered, I suppose. Then I sat down beside him on the wall and said, 'You told me your name was Jean-Paul, and we were supposed to meet in Brent Wood at three o'clock.'

'I know, I know.' His eyes were filled with terror again. 'But they stopped me . . .'

'The vampires?'

'They attacked me and left me . . . I didn't know where I was.' His voice fell away. 'I thought I was going to die . . .'

He was shaking so hard I gave his hand a little squeeze. 'Do you want me to get you help?'

'You can't,' he said simply.

'This afternoon you were going to tell me something.' I paused and waited.

He swallowed hard. 'They are planning something very bad, very soon, on the fifteenth. It is vital Marcus remembers who he is, as he knows—' He stopped and coughed. He really was in a bad way.

'Marcus knows how to stop them?' I prompted. But I don't know if Jean-Paul heard me, he was coughing so hard.

Then he leaned forward and looked right at me. 'Marcus *must* remember. I've tried so hard and failed. Now it is up to you. You are our last chance.'

'Me!'

'Yes, you must make his memory return before the fifteenth.'

'But it's the fourteenth tomorrow – well, today, in fact.'

'I know. Time is very short now. Have you something to help him remember?'

'You mean like a photo?' I said.

'That could work,' he said eagerly. 'Yes, a photograph.'

'Actually, there was one taken when I first met him at—'

I stopped. A big relieved, happy smile had just crossed Jean-Paul's face. But he wasn't smiling at me. There was someone else nearby, deep in the shadows. Someone I couldn't see at all yet – but he could.

'Could you help me up, please?' he said.

I did as he asked and then he said, 'You have been very kind, but I am not alone any more.'

'Who's there?' I asked at once.

'It is my mentor,' he said.

'You mean your teacher? But what's he doing here?'

'He has come to take me home so that I can recover from my attack,' he explained. Then he leaned forward, his voice low and urgent. 'Do everything you can to help Marcus regain his memory. But no more questions. Leave me now.'

'But you can hardly stand up.'

'I will be all right now, but please, please leave me.'

He was practically begging me not to follow him, so I just stood watching Jean-Paul stagger forward. While still shaky, he seemed a little more sure-footed now as he stumbled up Marcus's road. Then there was this swirling movement, as if the darkness had suddenly grown wings. And Jean-Paul disappeared.

He wasn't a deadly vampire, as I'd originally thought. No, he was a peace-loving half-vampire – I was certain of that. And when I'd seen him outside Marcus's house, he hadn't been casting a spell. No, he had been trying to break the memory spell on Marcus. But the deadly vampires couldn't have that. That's why Jean-Paul had been attacked so savagely.

Things were getting more dangerous all the time.

That's when I noticed something stir in the bushes. I was not alone. Something moved closer to me, making this swishing sound which sounded positively deafening in the darkness. Then I saw what it was – a big tomcat. I let out a huge sigh of relief. Cats are always prowling around at night.

This one didn't look very friendly, though, as he went on swishing his tail at me. He was a tortoiseshell cat, with huge green eyes. With a stab of horror I realized that I knew him.

That cat was called Rufus, and he had belonged to Mrs Lenchester – the most dangerous deadly vampire Marcus and I had ever encountered.

But Marcus and I had defeated her. That was humiliating for any vampire, but especially a deadly vampire. We'd assumed she'd be too ashamed to ever return. But did Rufus being here mean she was back?

Of course Rufus might just have a new owner. But it seemed unlikely, because he had been devoted to Mrs Lenchester.

The cat stared at me, arching his back now. Did he remember me? Once Mrs Lenchester had set that cat on to me. Was he about to try and attack me again?

But instead, the cat padded away. Was he going home to his owner? I decided to follow him.

The cat took off through Brent Woods. This place was a tangle of trees and spooky enough in the daytime; at night it was full of sinister shadows. But the cat was moving really quickly. So I didn't have time to feel very scared.

And then we were out of the wood and I could smell the tang of the river. We were very close to where Mrs Lenchester used to live. I crossed over the stone bridge and continued up this old road, full of expensive houses hidden behind huge trees. But right at the top of the road, aloof and mysterious, were two small cottages. They didn't fit in with the road at all and looked as if they had just landed there. The cat started scratching at the front door of the first house. This was where Mrs Lenchester had lived before, but now . . .

I waited impatiently. Suddenly the door opened a crack but no one seemed to be there. Someone must have been. I just couldn't see anyone. Then this mysterious figure closed the door again and the cat vanished.

I edged nearer, wondering if I might hear

voices. But there was only silence. And the cottage was in darkness.

Had Mrs Lenchester suddenly returned? Was she involved in this?

I went icy cold with horror then. She was truly to be feared.

# CHAPTER EIGHT

## *Trapped*

First thing next morning I found two photographs of Marcus. It wasn't hard. I knew exactly where they were.

They are the only pictures I've got of him and you can see his face in just one of them.

They were taken last October, not long after I started at my new school and met Marcus for the first time. I'd formed this secret society called 'Monsters in School' or M.I.S. People from my class sat around at night telling scary stories. And you were only allowed in if you were wearing a horror mask.

Marcus and his mate Joel just came along

for a laugh (as did most other people). But Joel took a couple of pictures of me with Marcus. In one of them we're both in our vampire masks, while in the other Marcus is holding his mask and acting silly as usual.

Joel printed off tons of pictures from that night. But these were the only ones I kept. And I really thought these could be the pictures to ignite Marcus's memory. They were so unusual for a start.

Marcus's parents might say I'm forcing him to remember. But I'm not. I'm merely giving him a massive nudge.

I decided I'd go round to Marcus's house straight after breakfast. I realized yesterday had been a complete disaster. But I was determined today would be totally different. For a start, *I'd* be totally different. I'd be friendly and nice. I was sure I could do nice. I was just a bit out of practice. (Thirteen years out of practice!)

I was gobbling down some toast when Glynis pushed her face right up close to mine. 'You're eating so fast – is that because you're off to see Marcus?'

'I am so not interested in this conversation,' I hissed.

'You never talk to me, do you?'

'Not if I can help it.'

'Why not?'

'Because it would only rot my brain.'

'You'd better be polite to me, as I know a huge secret about you, and if Mummy and Daddy knew it you'd be in big-time trouble.' Before she could say any more, Mum came in and she flounced off. My attention-seeking sister was always claiming she knew things, so it probably wasn't anything much. And I had far, far more important things to think about.

I walked quickly to Marcus's house. I was so determined this would be the day his memory at least started to come back. And absolutely nothing was going to stop me.

Only something did.

Just as I was walking briskly up Marcus's road, a car pulled up outside his house. Out of it jumped Gracie and a woman who could only have been her mum. So Gracie was visiting Marcus again. But she'd only seen him yesterday. I know I had as well, but I was here today on a vitally important memory-returning mission. She was only socializing.

Marcus bounced out, chatted to them both, and the next thing I knew the door had closed behind all three of them. Well, no point in my bursting in yet. Maybe Gracie and her mum were only visiting for a few minutes. Perhaps they were on their way off somewhere else. They might even be saying goodbye before they set off on a holiday – somewhere far away, hopefully.

I'd actually convinced myself that's what was happening when the door opened again. My hopes rose when I saw Gracie's mum leave. But they were thoroughly dashed when I saw her drive away alone. She'd obviously dropped Gracie off for the morning, if not the whole day.

So, absolutely no point in barging in there now – I'd just be the gooseberry who Gracie would occasionally try and drag into the conversation.

Worst of all, though, was how happy Marcus had looked when he'd opened the door to Gracie. If seven Christmas Days had arrived all at once he couldn't have been more chuffed. I bet Marcus wouldn't have looked like that if he'd seen me on his doorstep.

Once he might have done. But not now. Gracie was the one for him now. And even when he got his memory back, that wouldn't change.

I felt tears burning in the back of my eyes. Now I was being pathetic. The thing about people is, they're fickle. Every one of them. No point in getting upset about it.

I walked quickly away. Where was I going? Not back home, as Glynis would immediately jump on me, demanding, 'Why aren't you with Marcus? Doesn't he like you?'

But I just had to go somewhere, do something.

I decided to observe Mrs Lenchester's house and find out if she really *had* come back. That would definitely be something worth knowing – and help rescue this rubbish day.

The sun was out already, and spring was blossoming all around me. And yet a deadly vampire could be living less than a mile away.

As I walked through Brent Wood I had the prickly feeling that someone was following me. Once I was sure I heard a sharp rustling noise in the leaves. I whirled round. No one was there. Then I decided that I was so strung up from last night that I was finding enemies in every corner.

When I reached Mrs Lenchester's house I received a shock. In the daylight I could see that it looked totally different from how I remembered it.

Before, it had a neglected air with just a few thin parched-looking plants and a scraggy, sickly-looking tree in the front garden, and this had only added to the feeling that here was a place ringed around with danger and mystery. But today it shimmered and glowed with flowers. The front door had been painted too. Now it was a bright yellow colour. The whole house had been transformed and felt very much as if someone new had moved in.

All right, I'd seen Mrs Lenchester's cat Rufus last night. But cats often become more attached to places than people, don't they? So maybe only Rufus had returned to his old home.

I so hoped that was true.

I became more and more confident that it was. That's why I rang the doorbell. I was certain a totally new, completely harmless person would answer the door. I wouldn't go in, of course. No, I'd just babble some excuse and be incredibly relieved that at least we didn't have to deal with a really tricky, deadly vampire again. But instead no one answered the door at all. The curtains were only half drawn, so maybe the new owner was away.

But what a massive anti-climax. I really didn't want to just slink away. Then I noticed the back gate was open. Now my aunt in Eastbourne often leaves her back gate ajar when she's working in the garden and we all pile round there to see her. Was the new owner in the back garden too? Was that why it was left open so invitingly?

How about if I just knocked on the gate? So I did that and called out, 'Hi, is anyone there?'

And then I heard a voice say something. It wasn't very clear at all what was said – it was so old and gravelly – but it was an elderly man's voice. And I was sure he must have said, 'Come in,' so it would have been rude to just walk away.

I strolled round, fully expecting to see an elderly man weeding or planting. But there was no one. The garden, though, was spilling over with more bright flowers, and a blackbird started whistling in the trees overhead. It all looked so peaceful and innocent.

Then I noticed the shed. Sometimes my aunt in Eastbourne would pop out of her shed. The door was open as well so I knocked and peered inside. After the bright sunlight outside it felt very dark and gloomy in here, with just one small dusty window in the corner.

There was a clutter of garden tables and chairs, an ancient-looking lawnmower, spade, and a huge box with a blanket over it. And right in front of that box stood a very, very frail-looking old man, glaring at me with utter hatred. His expression left me in no doubt at all that he hadn't really said 'Come in,' to me.

'I'm extremely sorry to bother you,' I began.

He slowly raised a fist at me. He might

have been ancient but he was still dead scary.

'I'll just go,' I said hastily.

He called out something else. That wasn't clear either, but it didn't sound in the least friendly. At the same time I saw a flicker of movement deep in the roof of the shed. Something was up there.

A bird? Oh, let it be a bird . . . even a mad seagull would be preferable to what I feared it was.

Its wings twitched again. And then I could make out the rest of it: a small, dark, wizened little body hanging upside down and keeping spookily still, except for the occasional movement of its wings. I turned to the old man. But he'd gone, vanished into the darkness. That must mean he was a . . .

I knew then that I had to get out of there, fast!

I tell you, I was at the shed door in two swift strides. But I was too late. The door had already thudded shut, the sound echoing through the shed. I hammered and hammered at it. But the door hadn't only been shut – it had been firmly locked as well.

I turned round to see a shadow rising up out of the darkness. I stared at it for a moment, transfixed with horror. Then I realized that the vampire bat wasn't alone. Five or six other bats – hard to tell exactly how many – just erupted out of the air. Then they faced their target – *me*.

# CHAPTER NINE

## *Nothing Could Save Me Now*

Exactly as if they'd rehearsed it, all the bats started fluttering and flapping their wings together. They were like a gang revving up their bikes before they charged into action. Then they started letting out these horrible, spine-shivering howls too. They were exactly like the sounds I'd heard a few nights ago. Only these were even louder. They were like battle-cries.

I started madly pushing and pulling at that door again. I yelled out 'Help!' too, just for good measure.

If only I'd told someone where I was going.

If only Marcus were here with me.

I wondered suddenly what he'd do now. He'd probably say something really stupid like, 'Hey, bats, you're so bat-tastic, you should all go on *Britain's Got Talent*.' I could actually hear him saying that. But he'd also say, 'You're in a shed, so at least arm yourself.' Of course!

Just as I'd grabbed a spade the bats all shot forward and dived right at me. I started brandishing my spade as if it were a sword, swinging it about while this mad frenzy of whirling wings swarmed around me. The foul, rotting smell they gave off was so terrible it made me want to retch. But I didn't have time to be sick, as a bat had already landed on my face, its wildly flapping wings ruffling my hair.

I suddenly remembered the garlic that I always carry with me. I was reaching into my pocket, while still waving my garden spade about, when three more bats flew right into my face. It happened so suddenly I lost my balance. I just managed to stop myself from falling over. But the spade went clanking to the ground.

I was half on the ground too, and utterly defenceless, when I suddenly remembered this was the one morning I'd forgotten to pack any garlic. Well, I'd thought I was only going to see Marcus. Not that it would have been powerful enough to quell all these bats – who now lunged at me with their full force.

I fought back desperately, trying to pull them off me. But then I felt such a sharp, excruciating pain I cried out – I just couldn't help it. One of the bats had bitten right into my ear! I had to shut my eyes for a moment, the pain was so intense, but I knew I must keep on batting them away. There was no other way. It was getting harder and harder though, especially as one was holding onto my neck tightly, its teeth really digging in.

Somehow I managed to slam my fist right into it and send it spinning away. Meanwhile more were settling on me. There were just so many of them, and they were strong and fast and pretty much unstoppable. But I wasn't going to give up. I couldn't. But then another dived down into my face, so hard and fast that I totally lost my balance again and this time I fell to the floor.

They all just stormed onto me then as if sensing victory, while the whiff they gave off as they whirled excitedly over me was even worse. I really was going to throw up – if I didn't pass out first.

Nothing could save me now.

That's the last thing I remember thinking before the shed door slid open just a crack. Light trickled in, as did a voice. 'Oh no, this is awful. You must all stop at once.'

It was a soft, fluttery voice, but the bats obeyed instantly. An eerie stillness then hung over the shed, and the only sound was of footsteps slowly plodding towards me. And then that same voice said, 'Is this any way to treat a guest, who also happens to be an old friend of mine? I'm ashamed of you all.'

Then she crouched down and, smiling like the world's most adorable granny, ever so gently helped me up.

'Now, dear,' she said, 'I think it's time you and I had a nice cup of tea.'

I looked up into the eyes of Mrs Lenchester.

# CHAPTER TEN

## *The Golden One*

I was still so dazed with shock that I let Mrs Lenchester guide me through the back garden and into the house before I realized what I was doing. She was murmuring, 'I expect your knees are still a bit shaky.' (They were.) 'Well, that's only to be expected. So don't be afraid to lean on me. I'm stronger than I look.'

Laughing softly now, she led me past the kitchen and into a room I remembered very well – her sitting room. It was like a terrible nightmare suddenly finding myself here again. There was all the heavy, dark furniture and the marble clock, with its loud, slow ticking noise, while scattered all over the room were fading black and white photographs in silver frames of Mrs Lenchester with her late husband, Fergus, when they had acted on the stage together. Yes, everything was just as before, except the room seemed even more cluttered now.

Surely those huge, hideous lamps were new, as were the half-drawn velvet curtains, and definitely new was a large, very flattering painting of Mrs Lenchester and her husband in their theatrical heyday. There was something oddly familiar about him, but I couldn't put my finger on it just yet.

Mrs Lenchester, in a bright, patterned dress and more gaudily decorated than a Christmas tree – she was just dripping with jewellery – motioned for me to sit down on the green sofa, which looked even more spectacularly shabby than I remembered.

Last time I came here Mrs Lenchester, leaning heavily on a stick, had sunk down onto a chair too. But today she didn't sit down and didn't appear in need of a stick either. She looked much younger too. Well, some of her lines had definitely vanished.

Her eyes still looked old though, sinking right back into their sockets.

She leaned over me. 'I'm so sorry about that little misunderstanding.' Her honeyed words fell on me like a shadow. 'Unfortunately you were somewhere no human is allowed, ever.' It seemed very odd they were so protective of an old shed which had nothing in it at all really. 'You were warned off,' she went on.

'But I couldn't understand what the old man said.'

'Oh, couldn't you?' said Mrs Lenchester. 'Well, never mind, no harm done.'

'Who is that old man?' I asked.

She gave a brief, flashing smile. 'I shall have to find out and give him some elocution lessons.'

But she knew who it was. She *had* to know.

Then she added unexpectedly, 'Next time we meet I hope I shall be able to tell you all about him.'

Next time! So she was going to let me go . . .

I still felt a bit woozy, but I knew I should totter out of here as fast as I could. Yet I had a few questions which were burning inside me. 'Those vampire bats who attacked me . . . are they all staying in your shed?'

Mrs Lenchester fingered her necklace for a moment and then smiled coyly, like a shy schoolgirl who's just been asked to dance. 'Aren't I lucky? After I lost Fergus,' she said, staring up at the skeletal, gaunt-looking man in the portrait with her, 'I was very lonely. Sometimes I think loneliness is the scariest thing there is. Now, though, I have so many youngsters close by who look to me for advice – and guidance.'

I realized that by 'youngsters' she must mean young deadly vampires. Just like Marcus and I had feared, there were more and more of them arriving. 'Guidance about what?' I asked.

'The future,' said Mrs Lenchester vaguely. 'They're in and out of here all the time as well, running so many little errands for me. Nothing is too much trouble, and they're so enthusiastic. Naturally, they can get carried away sometimes.' She gave a fond chuckle.

'I suppose they got carried away last night when they attacked Jean-Paul,' I snapped.

Mrs Lenchester sighed heavily. 'I'm afraid they did. But that young creature was becoming excessively tiresome. He was even trying to communicate telepathically with your so-called friend to help him regain his memory. We couldn't have that, of course, so we had to give him a tiny little warning.'

'*A tiny little warning?* Poor Jean-Paul could hardly walk by the time they'd finished with him.'

Mrs Lenchester couldn't have looked more delighted.

'Why didn't you want him to help Marcus get his memory back?' I asked.

'I shall try and answer all your questions just as soon as we've had our tea. You must be gasping for a cup. I know I am.' She moved over to the table on which sat a huge silver teapot.

'No tea, thanks,' I said.

Mrs Lenchester looked surprised and hurt, and then gave an odd kind of chuckle. 'It's not drugged or anything, my dear, if that's what you're worried about. After all, if I'd wanted to hurt you I could have just let my over-enthusiastic young friends in the shed continue. But you're far too important for that. And I have very exciting news for you.'

I raised a sceptical eyebrow.

'No, really, you are going to be utterly thrilled when I tell you.' She gave another chuckle. 'I know, I'll let you choose which cup you have as they really are both the same.'

I chose the blue-flowered cup on the right. Mrs Lenchester took the other one and took a small, delicate sip of tea, then watched me do the same, while laughing delightedly. I marvelled again at how much younger she seemed. As if reading my thoughts she said, 'Looking well, aren't I?'

I had to admit she was.

'I remember feeling tired, too tired for words most of the time. But now the years are just falling off me.'

I put my tea down. It was very sweet. 'And that's all thanks to human blood, I suppose.'

'Oh, entirely,' she said. 'Of course, it's a bit like taking medicine, but it's done me the power of good – and its benefits go on and on . . .' She was now looking directly at me, her head tilted slightly. 'I told your so-called friend' – she spat these words out contemptuously – 'we'd return in triumph, and finally we—'

She stopped abruptly. Sunlight, which had been softly, respectfully peeking into the room, suddenly came flooding right in. The whole room seemed to shudder with horror as the sunlight showed it up for what it really was: a cross between a junk shop and a time capsule. No computer or laptop in here, not even a television. Everything seemed out of date, out of time. The modern world was barred, completely shut out.

It was then that I noticed how deathly quiet it was. None of the usual sounds from outside, like the swish of traffic. Even the birds had stopped singing. It was as if they were all suddenly still and silent on their branches, while waiting for . . . what exactly?

Mrs Lenchester stalked over to the curtains and pulled them shut. And then I felt something brush past my face. It was the lightest touch, but I knew for certain that something else was in this room too.

Right then I felt even more terrified than I had in the shed, without quite knowing why.

'I've got to go now,' I said. I tried to sound confident, assured, but as I said this a trembling fear began in my knees and then rushed through my body.

Mrs Lenchester stood over me, smiling. 'I'm afraid my visitor has alarmed you.' She pointed into the corner of the ceiling. 'Come on, show yourself.'

At once, dark wings began to flutter.

'Don't worry, it's not the angel of death.' Mrs Lenchester gave a loud cackle of laughter. And then she held out a hand. Immediately a bat soared onto it, just like a tame bird. 'The young like to stay so close to us.' She went on, murmuring at the bird, 'But you've frightened my important guest. So go away, you nosy little devil.'

The bat immediately swooped off her hand and disappeared.

'He's so curious, they all are, as to why I've allowed a human' – Mrs Lenchester's face immediately became pinched and hard – 'into my home. But I've been waiting for you.'

'Waiting for me?' I said.

'Oh yes, I sent Rufus to you as my emissary. Of course, I did think you'd knock on my door, rather than sneak about in my shed. But no matter, you are here.'

I was about to say again that I had to leave when Mrs Lenchester added unexpectedly, 'How lucky you are not to be anything like dull, ordinary mortals. You've tried your hardest to fit in with them, haven't you?'

Do you know, I almost, *almost* nodded in agreement.

'Humans look at you as if you're a person from another world, don't they?'

This time I couldn't stop myself nodding. But how on earth did she know that? It was as if she could see right into my life. I was impressed, despite myself.

'Well, keep trying to fit in if you want, but all humans will ever do is crush out your uniqueness. The only place you really belong is here, with us.'

That was a terrible, shocking thing to say. But I wasn't quite as shocked as I'd expected (or should have been). 'Only we can give you a truly precious gift,' she continued. 'Only we can help you be everything you really are.' She was standing right in front of me now, looking grave. 'As you are one of the golden ones.'

'The golden ones . . . ?' What rubbish was this now? Of course, I didn't believe a word Mrs Lenchester was saying. But she could tell a good tale. And I was kind of intrigued. So I just added, ever so lightly, 'Now who on earth are the golden ones?'

'The humans who aren't at home in this world at all. They're usually isolated – like you – and they often come down with strange, mysterious illnesses, as I know you have. That's their whole body rebelling against the human way of life and wanting them to use all their untapped magic powers.'

'You're saying,' I said slowly, 'that I have got magic powers?'

'Of course you have. In fact, you resonate with magic – but you don't believe me, do you?'

'Not in the slightest.'

'Well, let me give you a brief demonstration now. Stand up, dear, and prepare to be thoroughly amazed.'

# CHAPTER ELEVEN

### *Making Magic*

I got to my feet very warily.

Mrs Lenchester lumbered over to her mantelpiece, which was covered with ornaments. She picked up a small box and slowly walked over to me. Then she opened the box and brought out a tiny gold charm, the kind you might find on a bracelet. It looked very old and had little diamonds round the edges. 'Stretch out your right hand,' she said, and then she handed me the charm. 'Hold it and clench it as tightly as you can.'

Should I be doing this? I really didn't know.

But I was very curious – and yes, I'll admit it, very excited.

'Now go on holding it,' said Mrs Lenchester, 'while thinking of nothing.'

That was hard, especially with my heart hammering away. And all the time I was saying to myself, *I know you're intrigued, but be on your guard. You can't trust her*.

Mrs Lenchester had gone very still, and her voice was barely above a whisper as she said, 'Now repeat, *I am the golden one*.'

'I am the golden one,' I said.

'Now say it as if you mean it.'

'I am the golden one,' I said again.

'Next, continue holding the gold charm in your right hand and click your left hand as hard as you can.'

This all seemed fairly harmless. So, very cautiously, I obeyed her instructions.

'And now say, *Fire form*.'

The very second I did this, the fingers on my left hand started moving on their own, as if they didn't belong to me any more. They began twisting and curling all by themselves. And then tiny blue flames flared up on the edges of each one of my fingers. They flickered there like miniature candles, only lasting for a second or two. But it was truly incredible.

'Want to do it again?' asked Mrs Lenchester.

'Yeah, OK,' I said, fighting to keep the excitement out of my voice.

'Well, you know what to do, and keep gripping the gold charm in your right hand.'

So I clicked my fingers and said, 'Fire form,' much more confidently this time. Once again my fingers wriggled and writhed. And then a great burst of blue flame rose from my fingertips and swooped around the room, flying right up to the ceiling, where it blazed, before disappearing.

After it had gone I gasped, 'I did that.' I was just so amazed and delighted I had performed magic. 'It wasn't real fire, though,' I said.

Mrs Lenchester gave a small smile. 'No, it was an illusion, like most magic. But with practice you can do much more.' Her voice rose enthusiastically. 'With practice you could release and send off a fireball right into the face of someone who annoys you. And humans do annoy you, don't they?'

'Oh, all the time.' I grinned. 'And I annoy them too, even when I don't mean to.'

Mrs Lenchester gave a great cackle of laughter which was oddly infectious. I started laughing too. 'Now tell me' – her voice was low and confiding – 'are there any humans who you'd like to receive a fireball?'

'There certainly are,' I said at once. 'Like all the stuck-up girls in my class for a start.'

Mrs Lenchester laughed again. 'That fireball might only last a few seconds, but it will scare them to death. And afterwards who will believe them about what they've seen? No one. But they will know you are someone to be respected.'

'And they won't make any more snide comments about me after that.'

'They wouldn't dare,' agreed Mrs Lenchester.

For a moment we both stood there, gloating at my new power. I had to shake myself. I couldn't get sucked into this. 'You'd better have the gold charm back now,' I said quietly as I handed it to Mrs Lenchester.

She snatched it away.

'Is it very valuable?' I asked.

'To you it is priceless,' she said. 'It would help you so much. A million humans could have held that charm and never made the tiniest flame appear, just as they would never have heard our vampire cry a few nights ago. *You* heard it, though, didn't you?'

'Yes, I did,' I admitted. I remembered wondering why the rest of my family hadn't woken up like I did. I had been right – I was the only person who'd heard it.

'That was like,' said Mrs Lenchester, 'our little test for you. That call got into your blood, didn't it? You had to go out that night – you couldn't resist it.'

She was right, I really couldn't.

'We thought you might find that young man outside your so-called friend's house' – I noticed then how she never said Marcus's name out loud, always referring to him just as 'my so-called friend' – 'and distract him for us. But much more importantly, it was our final proof that you are indeed one of the golden ones, those very rare humans with special magical powers. Of course, for now those powers lie buried within you. But I can help you develop them if you wish.' Her arm snaked round my shoulders. 'And you did feel a new power running through you, didn't you, my dear?'

Well, I couldn't deny that. To think I had special magic powers – me! And if I developed them, that would show everyone. Nothing my brother or sister did could match that. I was so elated and triumphant I felt as if I'd won fifty sports trophies and passed fifty exams, all at once.

Mrs Lenchester cooed softly in my ear, 'You will find yourself coming here to see me more and more. This is where your future lies, not with humans. You can't trust one of them.'

That was true. Even Marcus had let me down with his fickleness. But I must never forget I couldn't trust Mrs Lenchester either. And she might be making the whole thing up about me being a golden one. Probably was. Anyway, she wasn't some kind of benign magician. She was a mean, vicious, deadly vampire living off human blood. And the last time we'd met she'd tried to kill me.

As if reading my thoughts she said, 'We got off on the wrong foot, didn't we, dear?'

I nearly laughed out loud. That was one way of putting it.

'But it was your so-called friend who so infuriated me. From now on things between us will be very different. You have my word on that.'

Her word, I thought scornfully.

'That means more than you realize,' said Mrs Lenchester. 'Vampires do not love. We are incapable of such feelings – we leave that to humans,' she added scornfully. 'See how honest I am being with you now. That is because I respect you. And respect, once earned, lasts much longer with us than love does with humans. I think you have just seen for yourself how changeable humans can be.'

That gave me a jolt. I thought again about Marcus, about how we'd been so close before, and how he obviously wanted to spend so much more time with Gracie than with me now.

'Oh yes, we vampires don't miss anything, especially now, with so many young, enthusiastic helpers venturing out in the daytime to act as our eyes. That is why our respect is so valuable. And about once every fifty years I find a human I respect.' I wondered what had happened to the last human Mrs Lenchester respected. 'You are one of those very rare humans. You will gain my respect for ever if you do us one small favour now. Would you like to hear what it is?'

I still didn't trust her – of course I didn't – but I was incredibly curious, so I nodded.

'It's very simple,' said Mrs Lenchester. 'I, or rather we, do not want you to contact your so-called friend until after tomorrow, after the fifteenth.'

The fifteenth. There was something familiar about that date. Then I realized – that was when Jean-Paul had said the deadly vampires would be starting their terrible new plan. Tomorrow! I kept my face still and tried not to let her see that it meant anything to me.

I stood waiting for her to say more, but instead she said, 'That's all. We want you to stay away from him for today and tomorrow – that's just two days. Nothing else.' She saw my surprised face and chuckled. 'So really, all you've got to do, my dear, is absolutely nothing.'

'And after the two days are up?' I asked.

'Then you are free to spend as much time with him as you can endure.'

I pretended to be curious. 'So what happens tomorrow?'

'I will tell you all when you have earned my respect. I cannot say anything else now. So do you think you might grant us this small favour?' Her smile vanished and her eyes became very sharp and watchful. 'But I don't want you to give me an answer at this moment.'

That was another surprise.

'I know you need time to think about it. So say nothing rash now. But if you agree to grant me this small favour, would you be so kind as to call on me at about half-past four? Everything stops for tea in this house then!'

'OK,' I said slowly.

'In return I shall give you the gold charm.'

I let out a gasp.

'Oh yes, it will be yours – and I will also teach you exactly how to use it. And then you will have powers other humans can only dream of. You will truly be one of the golden ones.'

'And I just have to call round and say I

won't see Marcus until after the fifteenth?'

Mrs Lenchester had a real cat-about-to-get-the-cream smile now. 'That is all.'

'And if I don't come and see you?' I said.

Mrs Lenchester went very still again, fixing her wizened eyes on me. 'A thwarted vampire has rage inside him or her that you have never seen. We make very dangerous enemies. So never be foolish enough to underestimate us. Why, right now one of the people closest to you is next door.'

'Who?' I demanded.

But Mrs Lenchester ducked the question. 'Oh, they're quite safe at the moment. They're with my great-niece. Do you know, it might even be my great-great-niece – I'm so ancient.' She gave another cackle of a laugh. 'Though I don't look it any more, do I? Anyway, Andrea has moved next door to me. Wonderful to be surrounded by young people. And she's such a keen gardener. She very kindly set about improving my back garden first – worked wonders. She knew I wanted it to look special to welcome back—' She stopped and I looked at her questioningly, but she only said, 'Andrea is a glorious painter too.'

'Did she paint that picture?' I asked, nodding at the portrait of Mrs Lenchester and Fergus.

'Isn't it breath-taking?' gushed Mrs Lenchester. 'And now she's transforming her own front garden, with someone very close to you helping.'

That still didn't make any sense. 'But who . . . ?' I began and then I added, 'Is it Marcus?'

'How your mind does run on that young man. No, it is someone far more congenial. Perhaps you'd like to see. I hate to rush you out . . .'

'No, I want to see,' I said. I was worried and incredibly curious as to who it could be next door. And what were they doing there anyway?

# CHAPTER TWELVE

## *In Big Trouble*

In the hallway a cat started twining itself around Mrs Lenchester's ankles and purring affectionately. It was Rufus. 'Yes, Tallulah has come back to us,' Mrs Lenchester said.

Rufus stopped and stared at me. 'We're in rather a hurry now, dear,' Mrs Lenchester went on to Rufus. 'I'm sure you and Tallulah will have plenty of time to catch up later.'

Outside a girl was crouched down, planting a large rose bush in the front garden and saying, 'Yes, I think you've picked exactly the right spot for it. Thank you so much.'

'Oh, I know all about flowers,' piped up a

voice I knew extremely well. 'I'm in charge of the school garden. Well, me and another girl, but it's mostly me.'

*Glynis.*

But what on earth was she doing here? Fear and shock burned so brightly in me that I could only shout, 'Glynis!'

Glynis smiled triumphantly at me. 'You never expected to see me here, did you? I've been helping Andy.'

'She certainly has.' The girl stood up. She had long, dyed-black hair and thick black painted eyebrows that made her look like a startled doll. Her head was huge, seeming far too large for her stick-like body. She was smiling at me, but the smile never reached her very dark eyes.

'You're called Andy?' I said slowly.

'Well, I hate Andrea, so it's become my nickname,' she said.

I'd heard the name before of course. 'And you work at Mad About Monsters.'

'That's right, but just part-time,' she said quietly. 'I dabble in so many things.'

'She certainly does,' cooed Mrs Lenchester. 'A girl of extraordinary talents.'

Andy twisted her face into a smile as she bent down to say to Glynis, 'I shall remember all your wonderful ideas. Do call again soon.'

'Oh, I will,' said Glynis.

'And come and see me too next time, dear,' said Mrs Lenchester.

I never ever wanted that to happen, so I said quickly, 'We must go.'

'It's been so lovely catching up,' said Mrs Lenchester. 'Apologies again if some of my young visitors were rather over-exuberant.' Then she hissed right in my ear, 'And if you could call round about that little favour later I'd be so grateful.'

As soon as we were out of earshot I demanded of Glynis, 'What were you doing here?'

Glynis just replied gleefully, 'You're in such big trouble.'

'Why's that?'

'Because I know all about you.'

'What are you shrieking about?'

She lowered her voice. 'You've been sneaking out at night to meet Marcus — and don't deny it. I heard you. You're not very quiet, you know.'

'Yes, I am.' I was quite insulted – I was a professional vampire hunter.

'I stayed awake until you came back too – hours and hours later. I expect you and Marcus have a secret meeting place where he plants kisses on you.'

'You're talking rubbish,' I protested feebly.

'I was supposed to go for another swimming lesson with my third best friend, Emma, this morning. But I followed you instead. You were going to see Marcus until you spotted that girl going into his house. Is he two-timing you? You can talk to me about boys – I'm very knowledgeable.' She added, 'Then I followed you to that cottage, and once you went inside I saw Andy gardening and I decided to say hello. I suppose that old lady is Marcus's nan?'

'Not exactly,' I said vaguely. How on earth could I explain my knowing Mrs Lenchester? I tried to think of a likely explanation, but I couldn't come up with anything – I was still too stunned at seeing my secret world of vampires suddenly crash into my ordinary everyday one. 'She's just someone I know,' I said at last.

That was very weak but Glynis didn't seem

to notice or care as she burbled on, 'Your Mrs Lenchester' – I winced at this – 'seems very nice. And I really like Andy, even if she has got a boy's name. I'd hate to have a boy's name. I'm going to see Andy again.'

I stopped walking. I stopped breathing for a few seconds too. 'No, you're not to go there again.'

'I will if I want to. You can't stop me. I might even go there this afternoon. Yes, I will – unless you take me shopping.'

'I can't today,' I said quickly. I had far too much to think about.

'Well then, I'll have to tell Mum and Dad about you going out at night. They'll hit the roof,' Glynis added cheerfully.

'They won't believe you.'

'Yes they will.'

Yes, they would. I looked at Glynis. 'And I suppose you want me to buy you something.'

'Yes please.'

'Well, I haven't got much money.'

'Just bring everything you've got.'

'And if I do, will you promise to stop following me?' *And get a life*, I nearly added.

Glynis considered. 'If you stay a long time

with me in the shops, I might. And if you buy me a nice present, of course.'

Back home Mum had just heard that Glynis hadn't gone swimming with Emma. 'You told Emma's mum you were with Tallulah?' Mum's voice rose incredulously.

'Well, I was, wasn't I?' said Glynis, turning to me.

'She was,' I admitted.

Mum actually gasped. She couldn't contain her shock and pleasure when she found out that Glynis and I were going out *together* again this afternoon – shopping.

'All right, calm down, Mum, it's not exactly grounds for a public holiday,' I said.

'I'm just really pleased,' said Mum, 'that at last—'

'And so are we,' interrupted Glynis, positively gloating in her bit of power over me.

But I wasn't as annoyed as I'd expected. I was just too busy re-running this morning's extraordinary events in my head. And especially when Mrs Lenchester said I was one of the golden ones and had given me that brooch and I'd made fire appear out of the air.

Of course, I knew I couldn't trust Mrs Lenchester – she was a treacherous vampire, for goodness' sake.

But still . . .

But still, NOTHING. I really had to tell myself off. I wasn't one of the golden ones – they probably didn't even exist, and it was just one of Mrs Lenchester's big fat lies. So why did I find it so hard to believe that?

Because I desperately wanted to be a golden one, that's why. In fact, I couldn't think of anything better than having magical powers. And I bet Mrs Lenchester knew that.

How clever she was. Still, the fact that she had gone to so much trouble with me showed one thing. She really thought I was a threat to her plan. She thought I could help Marcus get his memory back. And when he did – well, together we'd stop whatever the deadly vampires were planning for tomorrow.

But there really wasn't much time.

So while Glynis was changing yet again (she couldn't possibly go out in the same clothes in the afternoon as she'd worn in the morning), I rang Marcus. I told myself I really didn't care if Gracie was still there. It was beyond urgent now. Today was the fourteenth so he *had* to get his memory back or something terrible could happen tomorrow!

But I got a really unpleasant surprise when Gracie answered Marcus's phone. What was all that about? But somehow I swallowed down my intense irritation. 'It's Tallulah,' I said.

'Oh, hi there,' said Gracie. She didn't sound as gushingly friendly as usual.

'I'd like to speak to Marcus,' I went on.

'OK, sure, I'll try and put him on.'

What did she mean, 'try and put him on'? I could hear people talking in the background. They were out together somewhere, and it sounded like a café.

Gracie came back on the line. 'Sorry, but Marcus is really busy right now. Could he ring you back later?'

My heart stopped. 'Tell him . . . tell him any time this year would be just fine.'

I rang off.

Who did Gracie think she was, telling me Marcus was 'really busy right now'?

And really busy doing what exactly? Eating a bun, holding hands with Gracie? I bet when he heard it was me ringing, Marcus sighed heavily and said, 'Oh, not that loony again, just get rid of her somehow, Gracie.' And he couldn't even be bothered to give me the brush-off himself. He got Gracie to do his dirty work for him. That was beyond mean. No wonder I felt as if I'd just been kicked in the stomach. And that pain hurt me far more than when all those bats attacked me. This went right inside me.

Suddenly I started to laugh bitterly. All Mrs Lenchester wanted me to do was to stay away from Marcus for the next two days. Well, right now he was doing a pretty good job of achieving that all by himself.

Let him go on doing that.

I didn't need Marcus.

And I didn't care what the deadly vampires were planning for tomorrow either. You can get a bit sick of saving the world. Again.

But was I really going to drop in on Mrs Lenchester today for afternoon tea?

She'd promised me the charm if I did.

I started pacing around my room until Glynis burst in and started darting about like a mad wasp. 'Can we spend the whole afternoon shopping? You haven't got anything else to do, have you?'

'Not a thing until about half-past four.'

'And then are you going to see Marcus?' she demanded.

'No, I'm dropping in on Mrs Lenchester again.' I'd just said it aloud as a kind of dare to myself, hadn't I?

Now, as I write this, I want to shout out a warning, to shake some sense into myself.

Anything to stop me making the biggest mistake of my life.

# PART TWO

*Marcus*

# CHAPTER THIRTEEN

### *The Scariest Toy Ever*
### Thursday 14 April

#### 7.05 a.m.

I'm back.

And right now I'm getting so high on excitement I can't stay still. You see, when I woke up today (I'm waking up so early these days. Weirdly, I seem to need far less sleep than I used to) I actually remembered something.

I kept a blog.

And I began it on 30 September, the day of my thirteenth birthday (and the date when my memory blackout starts). I wrote acres of stuff in it too.

This is undoubtedly the biggest discovery since penicillin – well, practically.

I hate the way six months of my life have just disappeared. Especially as it feels as if part of me has vanished with them, and I'm not completely here right now.

But that's all over. I'll just have to read my blog and then I'll be up to speed on everything. Happy endings all round.

I've remembered something else. There's no stopping me now, is there? I kept my blog hidden behind top-secret passwords, so I must have some dead exciting stuff locked away there.

More soon.

### 7.20 a.m.
I can remember everything about my blogs except what the top-secret passwords are. Isn't that typical?

### 7.25 a.m.
I think I've remembered. I bet I used the opening letters of my favourite James Bond film.

### 7.28 a.m.
No I didn't.

### 7.29 a.m.

I didn't use the opening letters of my second favourite James Bond film either. Or my third.

### 7.31 a.m.

But I shan't give up.

### 8.22 a.m.

I've just given up. For one whole hour of my life all I've done is try and remember those wretched, stupid . . . no wonder my head aches like crazy. And I'm still no wiser.

### 8.45 a.m.

I've just asked my parents how much longer my amnesia is going to last. Do you know what they said? 'Oh, we never use the word *amnesia*.' They didn't care for 'mental black-out' or 'massively forgetful freak' either.

'No,' they said, 'this is just a little hiccup.'

A little hiccup which has lasted a whole entire week.

A little hiccup which is sending me insane with frustration.

A little hiccup . . . well, you get the idea. But

right now my mum and dad are the King and Queen of Relaxed about it all. They're putting on a top performance, I'll give them that. The trouble is, I know it is a performance, and I'd much rather they were honest with me.

### 9.05 a.m.

In the fridge I've just found a little bottle of a red drink which looks exactly like . . . well, blood. I was still examining it when Dad popped up. His eyes bulged out of his head when he saw me. He quietly said that this was his medicine.

'You can actually drink that?' I said.

'Oh yes,' he said.

I asked him to prove it. So he did, then he smacked his lips and pronounced it 'delicious'. He sounded as if he meant it as well.

'What crazy medicine,' I said. 'It looks exactly like you're drinking blood.'

We both had a bit of a laugh about that. But all the time he was laughing, Dad's face was as red as that bottle.

### 9.20 a.m.

Gracie's on her way round again. Seeing

her has definitely been the one – the only –
highlight of the past few days.

### 12.45 p.m.

You'd think losing a chunk of your memory
would be the weirdest thing that could happen
to you, wouldn't you?

Well, it isn't.

Not any more.

The moment Gracie arrived she seemed
different. Mum and Dad were wittering on
to her about the plans for their new kitchen
and she didn't even pretend to be interested,
as she normally would (Gracie is awesomely
polite). She just sat downstairs in a total daze.
Not like Gracie at all.

Then, after Gracie's mum had gone (she
was fascinated enough by the new kitchen for
both of them), Gracie tore upstairs and asked
me something really odd. 'How are you getting
on with your Jack Russell?'

I grinned. 'Well, a china dog is quite a res-
ponsibility. But I take it for walks every day.
You should see it out on its tiny little lead.'

But Gracie didn't smile. 'Do you like it?' she
rushed on. 'What I mean is, some toys have a

happy vibe – most do, I suppose – but a few just don't.'

'Is this a happy dog?' I asked, still not taking Gracie seriously at all. I picked it up. 'Well, let's see.'

And that's when something truly odd happened.

I was just glancing very casually at those black painted eyes when its expression seemed to change. All at once it looked fierce, almost as if it were warning me not to move it any more. Funny the tricks imagination can play on you, I thought.

I noticed too how it felt surprisingly warm. It must have caught the sun where I kept it. But then the toy dog started to get warmer. How was that possible? It wasn't. It couldn't get hotter all by itself, unless ... I looked under it, I pulled at it. Not a sign of a battery anywhere.

There had to be a completely rational explanation for this. And while I was wondering what it was, the dog went on getting even hotter. In fact, now I was juggling the dog from one hand to the other, just as I do when I'm holding hot chestnuts or something.

Finally I couldn't hold onto it any more. And it bounced – you might say jumped – out of my grip and onto the carpet.

Gracie was smiling faintly. 'Stop messing about,' she said.

'You're not going to believe this,' I said. 'I'm not totally sure I do myself, but that dog has just scalded me.'

Her voice rose. 'You are joking!'

So then I held up my hands and let her see just how red they were. A look of total horror crossed her face. 'Oh no, what have I done?'

Before I had time to puzzle over what she meant by that she sprang forward and picked up the Jack Russell.

'Be careful!' I cried at once. I mean, how absurd was that? Be careful picking up a toy dog!

Gracie's face had a look of grim determination on it. 'It *is* hot,' she began, 'but not too—'

'You just wait.'

Then the dog began wriggling about in her hand. 'Marcus, this is . . .' She let out a yelp of pain.

'Let it go!' I shouted.

The next moment the dog went flying out

of her hand. Considerably shaken, Gracie sat down on my bed.

I stood in front of her. 'Are you all right?'

'A bit shocked.'

'That dog's hot stuff, isn't it?'

Gracie didn't answer. She was just staring at the carpet.

'The thing to remember,' I said, 'is that it's just a china dog, so there's got to be—'

'No, there hasn't,' she interrupted, while peering even more intently at my carpet. 'Not if it's a *bewitched* china dog, which it is.'

'You never told me that.'

'No, I didn't, did I? I bought it at Mad About Monsters.'

'And they said about it getting hot . . . ?'

'Oh no, they said something quite different.'

'Now I'm totally confused,' I said.

'I only went into Mad About Monsters because people were handing out leaflets saying how everything was half price.' Gracie was talking as if she were confessing to a crime – and very quickly. 'And right by the entrance was this girl with huge, staring eyes, and behind her were all these Jack Russell dogs. She made a big fuss of me, so I thought she must be desperate for a sale. Then she said the Jack Russell I should buy was the one with the jet-black eyes, as this one was bewitched.'

Gracie paused for a moment, swallowed hard and then went on speaking even faster.

'She said, buy it for the person you like, and this dog will put a spell on them, making them shine with love for you. She said that any gift given with love has extra power too.'

She laughed then. So did I.

'I mean, I knew it was all rubbish,' she said.

'Of course you did,' I agreed. 'People will tell you anything to get you to buy stuff, won't they?'

'Exactly,' said Gracie.

'I'd probably have bought one as well,' I said, 'especially as they were half price.'

'Would you really?'

'Definitely.'

'Thank you, Marcus,' she muttered, still studying the carpet.

'What for?'

Gracie gave an odd little laugh. 'I don't

know.' She got up and stood gazing out of my window for a moment. 'I feel so ashamed,' she whispered.

'What are you talking about?'

She whirled round. 'I wouldn't normally have bought that dog, you know. But a couple of hours earlier you'd told me Tallulah was coming home soon, and when you saw her again you were going to ask her out.'

'I said that!' I was astonished.

'And I gabbled on about how happy I was for you both. Then I said I had to go home. Only I didn't go home. Do you know what I did instead? I sat in that little park near all the new shops and . . . I was so happy for you I started crying.'

'Hey, Gracie—' I began.

'No, don't interrupt. So anyway, after I'd finished feeling sorry for myself I dropped into Mad About Monsters, bought that stupid, spooky dog, and took it round to your house, making out it was just a welcome-home gift. You *are* the local superhero, remember? And you thought that was so great of me, when all the time I was trying to put a love spell on you . . .'

'But you didn't really believe it,' I said, thinking at the same time of what Gracie had called me – a local superhero. Wow . . .

'I honestly don't know what I believed,' Gracie was continuing. 'But then you had your accident, and since then you and I have never been closer, have we? Well, you don't remember. But take it from me, we haven't. While yesterday, when you saw Tallulah, it did not go well at all, did it!'

'No, but that doesn't mean I'm under a love spell.' I laughed a bit uneasily.

'I know, and I don't think you are. It's probably all just a massive coincidence. But normal china dogs do not get hot when you try and move them. And they break if you drop them too! So I have a horrible feeling I've brought magic – very bad magic – into your house. And for that I'm truly sorry.'

I went over to her. I was about to put my arm around her, but instead she burst out, 'We've got to get it out of your room now.'

'OK, I'll call the fire brigade,' I said lightly. I was making a not-very-funny joke, because I wanted to take the scare out of the situation. I looked again at the dog lying on the carpet.

If it had suddenly got up and run under my bed now I wouldn't have been very surprised.

No, I wanted it out of my bedroom too.

'How about,' I said, 'if I borrow Dad's thickest gardening gloves from the shed. Then I'll grab Hottie while I'm wearing them and lob it out of the window just as fast as I can?' I smiled. 'I don't know why I'm whispering. It can't hear us, can it?'

Gracie glanced over at it, lying in the middle of the carpet. 'I wouldn't put anything past that dog.' And her voice had dropped to a whisper too.

'Look, I won't be long,' I said, 'and don't feel you have to entertain it.'

As I walked downstairs, this whole thing seemed so incredible. A bewitched toy dog. I had heard, of course, of people putting spells on objects. Voodoo and all that. I knew it could be done, had been done. But those people had a reason for doing it. And usually they were taking revenge. But Gracie was just a random visitor to a shop, talking to a complete stranger. A complete stranger who claimed this dog could put a love spell on someone – on the very day I'd told Gracie about me asking Tallulah out.

The timing couldn't have been better. But that girl who'd sold Gracie the dog couldn't have known that, could she?

All these thoughts were tumbling around my head as I raced downstairs and out to the garden shed. I pulled out four drawers before finally finding Dad's thickest, grubbiest gardening gloves. These should do the trick. Then I stuffed them down my pocket as I didn't want my parents wondering why I was suddenly borrowing Dad's gloves. But they were too deep in conversation about new cupboards to be bothered about me. I sped back into my bedroom.

'Well, it hasn't moved or burned a hole through the floor,' said Gracie, 'but every second I'm waiting for it to do something else.'

'Time for me to fling this dog out of the window, then. It's just lucky that I am, in fact, the school cricket team's top bowler.'

'I never knew that.'

'That is a true fact.'

She smiled. 'No, it isn't.'

'Well, I'm sure it would be if I'd ever actually played cricket.' I was rattling away my usual rubbish, but actually I felt dead nervous. And as I approached the Jack Russell model I flexed my shoulders as if I were about to have a fight.

I sprang at the china dog – no snake attacking its prey could have moved more speedily – and snatched it up between two gloved hands. Then I dived for the window, which Gracie had already opened. Deep heat went coursing through my gloves, even with all that protection. In fact, it was agony hanging onto it. I very nearly let it drop again. But somehow I grasped onto it long enough to send it hurtling out through the window.

We both watched it bounce onto the grass. Then I slammed the window shut.

'Lock it too,' urged Gracie.

I did, and then she said, 'We mustn't leave it there. We must put it in the bin.'

'You took the words right out of my mouth,' I said.

Sadly, I am not one of life's action men. But right then I felt different – it must have been the shock, or Gracie calling me a superhero.

My head was suddenly much clearer and I knew exactly what I had to do.

We tore downstairs and onto the front lawn. The Jack Russell toy had smashed into two. 'Let me pick it up,' I said, as I still had the gloves on. I gingerly picked up its head. 'It's OK, not hot at all.' Then I grabbed the other bit.

'Put them in different bins,' whispered Gracie.

'You think together they might magically re-form?' I said.

'I just don't want to take any chances,' began Gracie, and then she hissed, 'We're being watched.'

And there was my mum walking over to us and saying, 'What on earth are you two up to?'

'Nothing much,' I said quietly. 'I just accidentally knocked this model dog out of the window.'

'Not the one Gracie gave you?' demanded Mum.

'The very same,' I said.

'Oh, Marcus,' cried Mum, 'how careless. But do you know, I think I might be able to stick it together for you.'

'No, don't do that!' cried Gracie and I together, so loudly Mum stared at us.

The thing is, Mum,' I said, 'we don't like to trouble you, especially when you're so busy with your new kitchen.'

Then Mum looked at me. 'Marcus, are those your dad's gloves you've got on?'

'Well spotted, Mum,' I said. 'And I've no doubt your next question is: *why*. Well, I'll tell you. It was all Gracie's idea – she wanted to see what I'd look like in Dad's gardening gloves, didn't you?'

'Yes, I did,' said Gracie, stifling a giggle.

'Who knows what she'll have me wearing tomorrow. Anyway, Mum, I've got an urgent appointment with the bin now.'

'And I'll go with you,' said Gracie. She sounded so eager, Mum gave us both another odd look before returning to the kitchen.

I scattered the remains of the dog into two different bins. Then Gracie insisted I put a stone on the lid of each bin. 'Just to make sure it can't sneak out and re-form tonight,' she said. She was smiling at herself as she said it. She went on, 'I'd hate for you to hear a tapping on your window tonight and then pull back the curtains and see that dog's face floating up at you.'

'Thanks so much for that, Gracie.' Then I added, 'But even worse would be if I woke up tomorrow and found it back on my shelf.'

'Oh, can you imagine . . .' began Gracie.

'No, I can't,' I said, 'because that china dog is broken, destroyed and no more.'

Gracie sighed, 'I feel so bad . . .'

'For trying to put a spell on me,' I teased.

'I don't think I'll ever admit to anything more embarrassing. Anyway, I won't be long.'

'Where are you going?'

Gracie seemed surprised by my question. 'To Mad About Monsters, of course.'

'After a refund, are you?' I asked lightly.

'I don't care about that. I just want some answers from the person who sold me that bewitched toy dog, because . . .' She hesitated.

'Go on.'

'Well, after I'd bought that wretched dog I didn't speed off to your house right away, as I felt a bit uneasy about what I'd done. So I went back to the shop to see who else was buying the dogs. They were still on sale but that girl had gone. Now I wonder if she'd just been waiting there for me.'

'But what on earth would be the point of selling one just to you . . . ?'

'That's what I'm going to find out. Bye.'

'So aren't I invited?'

'I suppose if you insist, I'll have to put up with you,' she said.

# CHAPTER FOURTEEN

## *Confrontation at Mad About Monsters*

### 1.30 p.m.

We half ran to Mad About Monsters. Outside the shop I said to Gracie, 'OK, are you ready?'

'Oh, I'm on fire,' she said. 'I don't think I've ever felt more determined.'

Herbert Cheshire – the eye-patch wearing owner – was unpacking some stock when we marched over to him. He greeted me lavishly. 'Ah, you've returned. May I hope we have made a convert to the wonderful world of horror?'

'Actually, it's my friend here who wanted a word with you.'

'Hello, my dear,' he said, bowing to Gracie. 'Herbert Cheshire, keen to help as always.'

Gracie, frowning, said, 'It's your assistant I want to see.'

'Andy,' he said.

'No, this was a girl.'

'So is she, but she likes to be called Andy. A long-standing nickname, I believe,' said Herbert. 'Alas, she isn't here today—'

'So where is she?' interrupted Gracie, a bit rudely.

'I really couldn't say, but she will be here all day tomorrow, as I have to go to London. But maybe I can help you now? I do hope so.'

'It's about a faulty toy dog,' she said.

'Faulty? In what way?' asked Herbert.

'It gets hot when you touch it,' said Gracie.

Herbert was looking very puzzled now. He sprinted over to the counter and picked up one of the little models. 'One of these dogs here,' he puzzled, 'gets hot when you touch it?'

'Not when you touch it – it's when you take it home and try and take it away from where it has been placed in the room . . .' Gracie's voice trailed away. It did sound more than a bit mad.

Herbert was picking up some of the dogs now and examining them while looking so baffled I wanted to laugh. 'But my dear, these are just ordinary toys.'

'The one I got wasn't,' said Gracie. 'Andy sold it to me as a bewitched dog. She said it would put a love spell on the boy I gave it to.'

Herbert's lips pursed with disapproval. 'Well, that was extremely naughty of her. And I shall have words with Andy about that. It may just have been a piece of charming whimsy on her part. But after hearing such claims I can see how you might imagine—'

'We didn't imagine anything,' said Gracie.

Then I noticed something. 'Hey, I remember I noticed this when I was here before – the eyes of the dogs here are different from the one you got for me. Mine had black eyes, not brown, and my dog's eyes glowed in the dark.'

'You must be mistaken,' said Herbert. 'All the dogs' eyes are identical.'

'This one wasn't.' Gracie and I said it together.

'Well, could you bring it in?'

A shudder ran through me. 'It's smashed up and in my bin.'

'And I'd hate to look at it ever again,' said Gracie.

Herbert cleared his throat. 'You know, nothing distresses me more than a dissatisfied customer, so please pick anything else in the shop you'd like – anything. And it is yours in exchange. See how I'm not even asking for any proof of purchase. I like to trust people—'

'No thank you, I don't want anything,' interrupted Gracie. 'I think there's something very dodgy going on in your shop.'

'And so do I,' I added.

Herbert looked affronted. 'But I repeat, these are merely little toy dogs – the most innocent creatures in my shop. And I know Andy would be most concerned if any comment she made to you, in jest—'

'She wasn't joking,' said Gracie. 'And if I were you, I wouldn't go to London tomorrow either. I'd *watch* her.' And with that Gracie marched off, leaving an open-mouthed Herbert Cheshire staring after her.

Outside Gracie said to me, 'Do you suppose he's in on it too?'

'Well, he's a very good actor if he is.' Then I smiled. 'I know one thing – I wouldn't like to get on the wrong side of you.'

'I don't normally get mad,' said Gracie, 'but I hate the fact that they've used me to get at you.'

I stared at her. 'But why should they – whoever they are – want to get at me? I'm nothing special, well, apart from my charm, good looks and overall modesty, of course.'

Gracie didn't smile, though. In fact, she looked dead serious before saying, 'I'm going back to Mad About Monsters later to interrogate that guy some more.'

For now, though, we decided to have a short break and visit the Hinton Tea Rooms. That place is as uncool as you can get, with all the waitresses in white blouses and black skirts and hushed conversations between the clinks of teacups. But the food is marvellous – especially all the home-made cakes, which you can choose yourself.

Gracie insisted on joining the long queue to purchase our banana cakes, while I bagged us a table. That's where I'm writing this and reflecting on the weirdest morning of my life and . . .

Wow. That was very odd. You know when you first get off a really fast fairground wheel and you feel all dizzy afterwards and a bit sick too? That's exactly how I feel now – and without going anywhere near a fairground wheel.

Now I'm feeling so dizzy I've got to stop for a bit.

# CHAPTER FIFTEEN

### *Ageing Fast*

**4.05 p.m.**

I went on feeling giddy and sick until I closed my eyes. And just as if I were sitting on a train looking out of the window, all these scenes flashed past. Only these were all fleeting glimpses from my mysterious recent past.

Finally one of the scenes slowed down. It was breakfast time. I was in the kitchen and my parents were telling me I had to take to school . . . a bottle of blood.

That didn't make any sense at all. And yet it sort of did too. I knew then that I was drawing close to a truly incredible secret.

But then that scene tumbled away too, and instead I saw something which seemed as if it belonged in a nightmare.

I was trapped in this dingy, dark room. Tallulah was there as well. And our captor was an evil old woman.

What on earth was going on?

And whatever were Tallulah and I doing here?

And that nasty old woman . . .

*Mrs Lenchester.* Her name just erupted in my head as I heard her saying to me, *Of course, the moment you arrived, I knew instantly what you were. If we're creatures of the night, what are you – creatures of the . . . when it's just starting to get dark?*

What was she talking about? She was making a stupid joke about me being a . . .

The words were in my head. But they were too far away. I concentrated like crazy. I had to hear this.

And then the words exploded in my head like a cork bursting out of a bottle. Now I knew what I was.

What I am.

# CHAPTER SIXTEEN

## *Incredible News*

# I AM A HALF-VAMPIRE!

# CHAPTER SEVENTEEN

## *A New Identity*

I stumbled to my feet. I couldn't sit still after remembering news like that. I couldn't walk very easily either. Not with my head shaking like crazy, because of all the memories, which were slamming into it now like bullets.

I WAS TOLD I WAS A HALF-VAMPIRE ON MY THIRTEENTH BIRTHDAY. TOLD BY MY PARENTS, WHO SHARED MY SECRET IDENTITY.

BUT THEY SAID IT WAS ALL RIGHT, WE WERE ONLY A BIT STRANGE. WE MIGHT LIKE THE ODD DROP OF BLOOD AND BE ABLE TO SHAPE-CHANGE INTO

BATS. BUT WE WERE COMPLETELY HARMLESS. NO HUMAN HAD ANYTHING TO FEAR FROM US.

I was blundering towards Gracie now. She was still in the queue. She gaped at me, wide-eyed with alarm. I tried to explain to her what was happening inside me. But it's incredibly hard to speak when your head feels as if it's about to explode. Then my mobile started to ring. I couldn't possibly talk to anyone now, so I just handed the phone to Gracie and then stumbled outside, where more memories were waiting to rush at me.

TO START WITH I HATED BEING A HALF-VAMPIRE, FEELING DIFFERENT, AND I JUST WANTED TO GO BACK TO BEING ORDINARY.

BUT THAT WASN'T A CHOICE I HAD. I COULD NEVER GO BACK.

THEN I STARTED TO GET USED TO MY NEW IDENTITY, ESPECIALLY WHEN I MET ANOTHER HALF-VAMPIRE – *GRACIE*. AND DISCOVERED I WAS ONE OF THE VERY FEW HALF-VAMPIRES TO HAVE SPECIAL POWERS, WHICH COULD RIVAL AND CHALLENGE THOSE OF ANY

VAMPIRE. SO I COULD SEND MESSAGES BY TELEPATHY, TRANSFORM INTO A BAT IN LESS THAN A SECOND AND FIGHT BRILLIANTLY . . . AND WITH THE HELP OF TALLULAH (WHO DOESN'T KNOW THE TRUTH ABOUT MY IDENTITY) AND GRACIE, I FOUGHT DEADLY VAMPIRES LIKE MRS LENCHESTER – AND WON.

THEN I WAS SENT TO FRANCE, TO ATTEND A SPECIAL TRAINING COURSE WITH THREE OTHER HALF-VAMPIRES. THERE I LEARNED HOW TO CALL UP AND CONTROL MY SPECIAL POWERS WHENEVER I NEEDED THEM . . .

'Marcus, are you all right?' Gracie was standing right beside me.

'The thing is, Gracie,' I announced, 'I've just aged six months.'

Her face changed instantly. All the concern went out of it. Now she was looking at me so hopefully.

'And you and me, Gracie, we're—'

She put one of her fingers on my lips. 'We never say the words aloud in public.'

'I know that,' I said, a bit indignantly. 'And I know that changing over into that thing we never say in public was worse for you,' I went on, showing off my new vastly improved memory, 'as you got all hairy – with hair spilling over your face. See, I remember all – or nearly all. The weeks in Paris are still a bit hazy, but everything else—'

'That's incredible.' She was beaming at me now. 'This is the best news. And it's just happened out of the blue – or has it?'

'The dog smashes – and my memory comes speeding back,' I said slowly.

'Do you think the shock of that dog turning all hot . . . ?'

'Jolted my memory back again?' I considered this. 'It could be, I suppose.'

Gracie peered at me. 'You still look a bit shaky, though.'

'Still feel it, actually. Well, I have got six months older in about ten minutes.'

'Shall we go and sit down somewhere, so we can both recover? Definitely not The Hinton Tea Rooms, though.'

'Why not?'

'Well, you did stumble out of there like Frankenstein's monster.'

I grinned. 'Do you dare me to stumble back in there like that?'

She grinned too. 'Oh yeah, definitely.'

So I did. I even added a couple of sound effects, just to add extra atmosphere. And soon Gracie was laughing so hard she was gasping for breath. I don't even know if I was as funny as all that. Maybe it was just relief that I was properly *me* again.

Anyway we stayed there for over two hours and I kept whispering to Gracie little things I'd remembered. Anyone listening to us would have thought we hadn't seen each other for months and were having a massive reunion.

Finally Gracie said, 'I suppose we'd better tell your parents what's happened.'

'The second we do,' I said, 'they'll call Dr Jasper and make such a big fuss and I'll be cooped up at home for the rest of the day. And I so want to see Tallulah first.'

The words were out of my mouth before I realized just how tactless they sounded. Telling one girl you really want to see another girl is never a great idea. Gracie didn't seem to react much, though, just asked gently, 'So you remember all about Tallulah now?'

And that was so weird, because it wasn't just that I remembered so much more about

Tallulah. It was as if I hadn't really seen her at all before. I mean, obviously I *had* seen Tallulah, but then it was as if she had been permanently out of focus. I suppose I just couldn't get past my first really bad impression of her. How could I have missed that she was funny, loyal and brave and so much else besides? I hadn't even properly noticed how dead beautiful she is.

'I suppose you remember asking Tallulah out now?' asked Gracie lightly.

'Yeah, I do,' I replied, equally lightly.

'That's good . . . By the way, you know when you were having all your flashbacks and you handed me your mobile . . . ?'

'Yeah.'

'Well, that was Tallulah and she wasn't at all pleased when I answered the phone. I think she thought you were ignoring her—'

'Oh, poor Tallulah.'

'So ring her now,' said Gracie.

I considered. 'No, much better if I explain face to face.'

'Well, you go and see Tallulah and I'll ring my mum to pick me up.'

I stared at her. 'You needn't think you're leaving now.'

'Needn't I?'

'No, you're coming to see Tallulah with me. And then we're going back to my house, and I really want you to stay over. Well, this is a big night and we've got to celebrate. Plus, my parents will be at me with a million questions so I want someone there with me. And that someone is definitely you.'

Gracie looked surprised but pleased.

**4.45 p.m.**

I still haven't seen Tallulah.

We went round to her house and it was Glynis, her little sister, who answered the door. She smiled sweetly at me, but practically snarled at poor Gracie.

'Hey, Glynis, is Tallulah about?' I asked.

'You've just missed her, Marcus,' she said. 'She's gone to see such a lovely old lady.'

And I nearly said, 'Well, ask her to call me when she gets back.' But something made me curious about this lovely old lady Tallulah was suddenly visiting.

'What's this lady's name?' I asked. 'Do you know?'

Glynis leaned in confidingly, totally ignoring

Gracie. 'Her name is . . . oh, what is it? Her great-niece has just moved in next door and she's really nice too. She said I had green fingers as I helped her—'

'The name,' I interrupted.

'I do know it,' said Glynis. 'It's . . . Mrs Lenchester!' she cried triumphantly.

I actually stepped back from Glynis in horror while Gracie let out a loud gasp. It was bad enough hearing that Mrs Lenchester was back. But that Tallulah had gone round to see her on her own . . . Why? What was she thinking of?

I asked hoarsely, 'Does Mrs Lenchester still live in that little cottage near the river?'

'That's right,' said Glynis.

'And you say her great-niece has moved in next door?' asked Gracie.

Glynis wrinkled up her nose when Gracie spoke. 'I don't think you should both go round. It'll be too much trouble for Mrs Lenchester. So just you go,' she said to me, and after frowning at Gracie she closed the door.

'Why on earth should Tallulah—?' began Gracie.

I lowered my voice. 'Tallulah's investigating deadly vampires, isn't she? Only on her own this time. And she's found out that Mrs Lenchester is back. Why? I mean, we defeated Mrs Lenchester, humiliated her . . . a deadly vampire would never return—'

'Unless they were planning something really big, and were totally confident of success,' said Gracie.

Suddenly I remembered something from my accident. 'The bat that the driver said he'd seen flying in front of his car, just before he hit me. Maybe my accident wasn't an accident after all. Not if Mrs Lenchester was back. Maybe it was done on purpose, to try and get me out of the way.'

Gracie nodded. 'And now I'm wondering if that weird dog was even more suspicious than we first thought too. Doesn't it seem strange to you that your memory came back just a few hours after it was smashed? Maybe it's all connected.' Then she looked hard at me. 'We've got to get Tallulah out of there.'

'I think we should run like death,' I said.

And we did.

# PART THREE

*Tallulah*

# CHAPTER EIGHTEEN

### *Another Gift*

Somewhere a clock is striking four o'clock in the morning. I've been writing for hours. No wonder my eyes are starting to feel so heavy.

But I can't stop now.

I have so much more to tell you and this is my very last chance.

So, back to the afternoon when I planned to return to Mrs Lenchester's. First, though, I had to endure going shopping with Glynis. We ended up in Bailey's, a so-called cool shop for teenagers. It had boys' clothes downstairs and awful, over-priced stuff for girls upstairs.

Just my luck that the girls' section was

teeming with the 'popular' set from my school that afternoon. They all made these weirded-out faces when they saw me daring to venture onto their territory. And one girl declared in a loud piercing whisper from a changing room, 'Her being here is just wrong on so many levels.'

'They're so rude to you!' said Glynis.

'And I'm reeling from that new experience,' I replied.

But I knew that I, in my baggy jeans and hoodie, with my unwashed hair all scraped back and not an atom of makeup on, could never, ever fit in with these 'beautiful' girls, preening in front of mirrors and prattling about boy bands. The distance between us was uncrossable, while the distance between me and Mrs Lenchester – that should be at least as uncrossable. But right now, in Bailey's, I had my doubts.

I watched Glynis capering about trying on all the hideous jewellery, when suddenly she said to me, 'These are in the sale – why don't you try them on?' And she handed me a pair of bright pink high-heeled boots. Not at all the sort of thing I wear, but just for something to do and to really give the girls from my school something to talk about, I grabbed the boots and put them on.

Actually they looked all right on me, in a totally bizarre sort of way.

Not that I'd ever waste my money on them. And by the time I'd finished paying for Glynis's terrible taste in jewellery I didn't have any money left anyway.

'That's it,' I said to Glynis after we'd left. 'You're not getting anything else from me.'

'Yes, Tallulah,' said Glynis, surprisingly meekly. Then she pressed a clammy hand into mine. 'And this is for you.'

'What is it . . . ?' I began. But then she handed me a bag, and before I even opened it I knew that inside would be those pink, high-heeled boots. I was so shocked I couldn't speak for a few seconds.

'You liked them so much,' she said. 'I could tell.'

'Thank you, Glynis,' I said quietly. Actually I doubted if I'd ever wear them, but still, I'd never ever expected that. And I was so shocked, so totally stunned – and, I'll admit it, so pleased – by my highly annoying little sister buying me a present that it jolted me back to my senses.

Was I really going to drop in on a highly dangerous, deadly vampire? So just who would I be calling on next – my good mate Darth Vader?

But ever since this morning I'd gone a bit insane. It was seeing Marcus looking so pleased when Gracie turned up at his house that had started it. One tiny moment which had passed by in a flash, but instantly I had been eaten up with jealousy. No, it was more than a touch of jealousy – it was as if I'd caught some awful disease which had made me shrivel up inside.

And Mrs Lenchester had spotted how I'd shrunk into myself and played on it. No wonder she was so certain I'd return.

No chance of that now, except . . .

And it was then that I had the biggest, boldest, maddest idea of my life. Why didn't I go back to Mrs Lenchester's house and let her think I was still all twisted up inside (I could do that) while playing on her one huge weakness – her vanity – to find out just what she and the other deadly vampires were planning?

She had very nearly told me before –
she'd so wanted to indulge in the ecstasy of
showing off. And this was positively my very
last chance to find out, as it was the fifteenth
tomorrow.

The whole idea was fraught with danger, I
knew that. But if I could pull it off, and find
out the deadly vampires' scheme – well, how
brilliant that would be. After which I'd immediately tear round to Marcus's house. I still
had photographs on me, so I bet I could make
his memory return. And together we'd stop
them.

And I didn't care if Gracie was still there.
In fact, I was happy about her and Marcus.
No, I wasn't. That was going much too far. But
Marcus and I would still share our vampire-
fighting missions together. No one could stop
that. And this mission looked like our biggest
yet.

I was getting so excited now.

And here's the thing about crazy ideas – the
longer you think about them, the less crazy
they seem, don't they?

So after I'd walked Glynis home I told her I
was now popping in on Mrs Lenchester. Glynis

looked kind of shy for a second and then asked if I'd be wearing my new boots.

'Sure, why not?' I said, handing her my trainers. And that's why I clumped off in totally ridiculous pink boots to try and outwit a deadly vampire.

# CHAPTER NINETEEN

## *Mind Rays*

I didn't even need to ring on the doorbell. Mrs Lenchester had obviously been waiting for me. She opened the door, then leaned forward and whispered into my ear, 'You've come back for the charm, haven't you?' She was convinced it was that which gave her a hold over me.

So I played along and said, 'It's all I can think about.' (And for a while, it had been.) She chuckled and completely believed me, I could tell. And do you know? I wasn't nervous at all. Not then. I was just so exhilarated. I can do this, I told myself, I can totally fool

Mrs Lenchester and find out exactly what's going on.

'That gold charm will give you undreamed-of powers. You were very wise to return,' she said.

'And power is everything,' I said.

Mrs Lenchester nodded approvingly. 'Now come in, my dear, the tea is all ready.'

Once more I sank onto her shabby old couch while she, smiling ever so cheerfully, handed me a cup of tea and a plate of home-made biscuits.

'I've baked them in your honour, so do try one first, dear,' she said.

I took one small bite out of one of the biscuits and immediately pronounced, 'That's truly delicious,' and actually it was.

She nodded, pleased. She loved compliments. Then her tone became more business-like. 'Now, you haven't seen him?'

'No, I haven't,' I could say completely truthfully.

'And you will avoid all contact with him tomorrow?' I could feel her jet-black eyes watching me really intently now.

'I certainly will,' I said. Then I added, 'That

won't be hard, as all his time is taken up with someone else now – this really simpering, silly girl.'

Mrs Lenchester's eyes lit up.

'You're quite right,' I went on. 'Humans are so fickle and very, very sly, and I'm sick of every one of them. That's why, whatever you're planning, I'd like to be in on it more than anything.'

Had I pushed it too hard now? Would she become suspicious?

Mrs Lenchester got to her feet. Her smile had vanished, and her voice was much lower. 'Your enthusiasm is admirable but I'm afraid that won't be possible . . . yet.' She emphasized that last word.

I pressed a bit more. 'But there's something very big happening tomorrow?'

'Oh yes,' said Mrs Lenchester.

'Even bigger than what you've done before?'

'Oh, much bigger,' said Mrs Lenchester.

I waited expectantly, breathlessly. I knew Mrs Lenchester could never resist such an appreciative audience. And she didn't. 'You know, my dear,' she began, 'we are survivors

– the only survivors – from the days when magic still ruled the world. Then that all disappeared. Oh, a few of us could stick pins in an image and make someone writhe in agony – inferior stuff. But now human blood has helped us not only to become younger and stronger but to reclaim our ancient powers of dark magic.'

I gasped in a highly impressed way. I was really close to finding out the plan now. But I knew I mustn't overplay it. That could destroy everything. So I just gazed at her, rapt and intent, knowing Mrs Lenchester was drinking in my attention.

Standing right in front of me now, she asked, 'Have you heard of death rays?'

I nodded, not even daring to speak.

'And you probably thought it was all far-fetched science fiction. But there's something which few comic books have ever portrayed. Something beyond, it seems, human imagination – *mind rays*. To be able to dig down into a human's mind and then smash away at their most prized possession, until you just leave a shell, a husk of a human being—'

'Do you mean their memories?' I blurted out.

'You're coming on,' cried Mrs Lenchester approvingly, half walking, half dancing around the room now. 'It is memories which make any human being what they are. Wipe them out and you destroy the person.'

I thought immediately of Marcus. As if reading my mind, Mrs Lenchester said, 'Yes, that's right. When we learned he had gone to Paris, it seemed like the ideal moment to return – without him around to mess up our plans once more. When he returned early we had to deal with him. We couldn't have him interfering with our plans, so although we weren't ready, we experimented with him.'

'Through that car accident?'

Mrs Lenchester was gleeful. 'That fooled you, fooled everyone, didn't it?

'Fooled me?' I stared at her questioningly.

Her eyes grew wider. 'We staged that car accident deliberately, so everyone would think that was how he had lost his memory and would focus on that, never suspecting what was really going on. That was, if you like, our red herring. The true cause of Marcus's memory loss was right under his nose all along.'

'You really are immensely clever,' I said coaxingly. I still had no idea what she meant, but I hoped she'd reveal the truth any moment now.

'And it's time we let humans see just how clever we can be,' said Mrs Lenchester.

'Well, they'll soon find out,' I said.

'They will,' said Mrs Lenchester, giving a strange high-pitched laugh. 'For your friend only lost a few months of memory – the vital ones, though, as far as we are concerned. But now we have the power to wipe out years and years – decades even – of anyone's memories. Best of all, we can destroy a human mind without being anywhere near that person when it happens.'

'But how on earth do you do that?' I asked.

'By letting our spell quietly seep into their lives through—'

'Yes,' I began, urging her on.

But then she stopped. She was staring past me. 'Oh, all right,' she said. I couldn't see who she was talking to, although just for a second I thought I glimpsed a shadowy figure in the doorway. Mrs Lenchester seemed distinctly chastened now as she sat down opposite me. 'I'm being told off for saying too much.'

'By who?'

'By the person who masterminded this whole scheme.'

'But I thought that was you,' I said.

She liked that, breathing in my compliment as if it were an exquisite scent. 'I am certainly a vital member of this scheme,' she said. 'But it is someone else who came up with the idea.' She smiled fondly for a moment. 'Someone who you've seen,' she went on.

Now, Andy was my number one suspect. In fact, the only one I could think of – unless it was . . .

Herbert Cheshire? Could he possibly be the secret vampire behind this whole scheme? I'd be so disappointed if he were, as I'd liked him.

I opened my mouth to ask something else, but she raised a bejewelled hand. 'No more questions.'

I wasn't altogether sorry. There was something about this shadowy figure – the so-called mastermind – which had really scared me. Well, he or she had even alarmed Mrs Lenchester.

I'd found out a lot and needed time to think about that and see Marcus. 'Thank you for the tea,' I said. 'But you must be very busy.'

Mrs Lenchester didn't disagree. The whole mood here seemed to have suddenly changed and become much tenser now.

We both got up, just as Rufus slunk into the room, padding across the floor to leap up onto the couch just where I had been sitting a moment ago. His green eyes glared at me.

Mrs Lenchester smiled at him for a moment, then looked up again at me. 'But aren't you forgetting something?' she whispered. 'Your charm?'

I really had forgotten all about that.

'I didn't think I'd be allowed to take that today,' I said.

'But I am very pleased with you. So I think you deserve a reward. And you *are* a golden one.'

And I knew that for a few hours I'd been practically hypnotized by that title. It seemed like I had been a different person then.

'Well, stretch out your hand,' hissed Mrs

Lenchester, smiling coyly at me. And into my outstretched hand she dropped the tiny gold charm. 'Look after it very carefully and bring it with you every time you come and visit me. Remember, too, whatever humans do to you, you've still got this charm. This will help you take revenge on them, and—' She stopped abruptly. 'Will you excuse me for a moment, my dear?' She hastily left the room.

Silence, save for the loud ticking sound of the clock and a grumbling sort of purr from Rufus. I glanced around at all the heavy furniture, which seemed to have suddenly moved closer to me – silly the things you can imagine. But then I felt a chill down my back and that *wasn't* my imagination. A vampire bat was hovering above my head. And then another one had joined it. I didn't like this at all.

'I'll have to go now,' I called out. No one answered. Fear descended on me like a gust of freezing cold air. Danger was flooding all through this room.

I started to walk to the door. And then Mrs Lenchester returned. Her face was very grim. She faced me, unsmiling. 'You fool, you stupid fool.' Her voice was like a whip. She moved nearer, but now talking as much to herself as me. 'And I trusted you. I actually let myself try and help a human.'

'But what have I done?' I cried, genuinely bewildered.

'You promised me you hadn't seen that boy.'

'And I haven't.'

'Liar,' cried Mrs Lenchester, raising her hand, and for a moment I actually thought she was going to strike me. But instead she just hissed, 'If you haven't seen him, what's he doing standing outside this house?'

'I don't know,' I cried. 'But I swear I haven't seen him today.'

Mrs Lenchester shook her head gravely at me. 'Right now I almost feel sorry for you.'

# CHAPTER TWENTY

## *The Biggest Mistake of My Whole Life*

'You might have been a part of this,' she went on in a choked whisper. 'Undreamed-of powers could have been yours, you foolish, foolish girl. Instead you have contacted that abomination.'

'But I haven't,' I protested. 'I—'

'I saved your life, you know. That day when you went nosing round my back garden despite being firmly told to go away.'

'But I really thought someone said, "Come in".'

'When you dared to invade our shed he was all for attacking and then experimenting on you.'

A shudder ran right through me. Was she talking about the old man I had seen there? Who was he?

'Only I could have got you out of that shed,' Mrs Lenchester went on. 'And I did, because I saw a spark of real magic in you.'

'Oh, this is all so sad,' came a rasping, mocking voice behind me.

I jumped and spun round. I couldn't see anything except a grey kind of shadow at first. But then the shadow began to take a human shape. And there was an extremely old man with very little neck, a shock of white hair and no expression at all. He was dressed in a white suit with a large pink bow tie. But his clothes hung loosely off him, as if they even they didn't dare get too close.

'I saw you in the shed that day,' I said. 'And I'm sorry I misunderstood you saying, "Go away".'

Even now I had to concentrate hard to understand his clipped, plummy voice. But he totally ignored me at first and said to Mrs Lenchester, 'What a display. *I saw a spark of real magic in you.* You are becoming as lachrymose as a human.' Mrs Lenchester actually dipped her head in shame. 'And I don't suppose you even know what lachrymose means,' he snapped at me.

'Yes, I do, actually! It means all weepy and tearful and wet,' I replied crossly. 'Who are you?'

'But surely you recognize him,' said Mrs Lenchester. She sounded shocked, even indignant. 'Look around at all my wonderful pictures.'

But her wonderful pictures were all just faded black and white photographs of Mrs Lenchester and her husband on their wedding day and in plays together and—

I stopped.

No, that was incredible. I looked again at the grizzled figure in front of me.

Her husband Fergus was dead, yet here he was back as a very aged . . .

'You're a ghost,' I said to him.

'Oh no,' moaned Mrs Lenchester.

'I am much, much more than a ghost,' rasped the man, clearly enraged by my comment.

'Of course you are, Fergus,' cooed Mrs Lenchester soothingly. 'You started as that, but now you're becoming more solid, more real all the time. And soon you'll be able to take vampire form again, and drink human blood, and we'll grow younger together.'

But he was still shaking with fury. 'Come here.' I edged cautiously towards him. Then he stretched out his hand to me. 'Well, take it,' he snapped. A dry, skinny hand was pressed into mine. 'Could you touch a ghost?' he demanded.

And as he spoke, sour breath touched my face. He really wasn't just a ghost. No wonder he was so furious when I had called him that. He was like some horrifying mixture – part ghost, part monster.

'I'm afraid you have been extremely stupid – even for a human,' he went on. 'You pretend you are following our instructions while all the time parading that abomination right in front of us.'

'But I didn't—' I began.

'You are becoming wearisome,' he said.

'Look, I just want to go,' I said.

'I'm afraid that's not a choice you have now. But don't worry, you won't be attacked this time. All you have to do is accept a small gift from us.'

'What kind of gift?' I demanded at once.

He ignored my question. 'We will need to prepare one in the shed. I shall have to go with Andy—'

'No, you won't.' Andy swaggered into the sitting room. 'We prepared a few earlier, didn't we?'

'Oh yes, of course we did,' said Mr Lenchester, speaking far more politely to her than to his own wife. 'Fetch one of our gifts, would you, please?'

'With pleasure.' A very ugly glint came into Andy's eyes as she said this.

After she'd left, Mrs Lenchester asked suddenly, quietly, 'Is there no other way?'

Although Mr Lenchester wasn't strictly a ghost, he moved like one, his feet not quite touching the floor as he flowed across the room to his wife, who was hovering by the door like a nervous waitress, and hissed at her, 'You refused to listen to me last time about that girl and look at the result.'

'All right, no need to go on and on about it,' said Mrs Lenchester. 'I thought I'd found a human who hated other people nearly as much as I did. I thought I'd found a human protégée. I was wrong.' She said this last word like a deep groan. 'But about her magical potential I was completely right, and I could have helped her so much.'

'Help me now, Mrs Lenchester,' I cried desperately, moving towards her. 'Let me go, please.'

'I can't,' she said, and turned away from me.

Then Andy returned and I saw what she was holding. A little model of a Jack Russell. The dogs they sold in Mad About Monsters. Like the one Gracie had given to Marcus.

'This is our gift to you,' said Andy.

'And you will be completely safe from any further attacks, if you accept our present,' said Mr Lenchester smoothly. 'We shall also have to ask you to avail yourself of our hospitality for a few more hours. But in the morning you will be free to leave and resume your life, provided you accept the gift now.' Then he said fussily to Andy, 'Hold the dog's head up a little more and clasp it very carefully now.'

As Andy walked towards me, her fake orange fingernails curled all round the dog, I shrank back. I just knew this gift was truly to be feared.

'No, I don't want it!' I cried. 'I won't accept it!'

'Why ever not?' asked Mr Lenchester, who was standing just behind Andy.

'Because – because,' I cried wildly, 'you've somehow twisted that model dog with your vile power.'

'Not twisted it,' said Mr Lenchester. '*Transformed* it. Why, this little toy can relieve humans of something which gives them so much pain and misery. You could say we're offering them – and you – some much-needed relief, by ensuring years and years of their memory are wiped out.'

But how could a china dog wipe out years and years of memory?

And that's when I noticed something – the dog's eyes. They weren't brown like all those in the shop. No, they were jet black, exactly like the eyes of the dog in Marcus's bedroom. Andy had said they'd prepared the dog earlier. That meant . . .

'You've painted over the eyes!' I burst out.

'That's what it looks like,' said Mr Lenchester proudly. He'd stopped walking towards me and so had Andy.

'Yes,' I said at once.

'My creation would not have been possible without the aid of my highly talented great-niece here.' And Andy actually gave a very deep bow.

'For some time,' he went on, 'a few vampires could cast a spell on innocuous, banál objects such as toys. But it was here today, gone tomorrow. Now, for the first time, that spell can be locked in like energy in a battery. I had the marvellous idea, but my fingers are too ancient and crumbling to accomplish such a delicate task. My great-niece here, though' – Andy took another bow – 'can fix any spell. And once the object is bewitched, its eyes actually change colour to black. Then we know the spell is there, waiting and ready to be activated by whoever accepts this dog as a gift.'

'And they can't do anything about it?'

'Not a thing,' said Mr Lenchester. 'In fact, they will be totally unaware a spell is quietly seeping into their life and rotting away their memories. The first the human will know about it is between twelve and fourteen hours later when they find their memories have all been drained away.' He chuckled. 'It was a gift to us when that girl came into the shop, and Andy knew how easy it would be to deal with that boy.'

'Never guessing the cause of it,' cut in Andy gleefully. 'Or realizing the only way to break the spell is to smash the dog. Not that this will be easy. The dog can be moved about easily enough, but it also contains a small device which means it will resist any attempt to separate it from its owner – or to destroy it.'

'And tomorrow?' I prompted.

'One thousand of them,' said Mr Lenchester, 'all of which will be prepared tonight, will be unleashed tomorrow morning on the fifteenth—'

'At Mad About Monsters,' I interrupted.

'Of course,' said Mr Lenchester.

'Is Herbert Cheshire in on it?' I asked.

Andy sniffed contemptuously. 'That terminally constipated human is just a big nuisance. He will be away most of tomorrow anyway. But before he goes I think I'll give him a little present, something for him not to remember us by.' She and Mr Lenchester laughed while

I thought, If somehow I get out of here and after I've seen Marcus, the very next thing I'll do is warn Herbert Cheshire of the real-life horror he faces in his shop.

'And,' went on Andy, 'I shall sell my dogs at such a cheap price that the gullible humans will snap them up, either for themselves or for their so-called loved ones.'

She and Mr Lenchester both looked so triumphant I had to cut in, 'But those humans haven't done you any harm and you're going to destroy their lives – and that of their families.'

'Yes, we are,' agreed Mr Lenchester without a flicker of concern.

'So why are you doing it?' I demanded.

He and Andy looked stunned by my question. To them it was like asking someone why you drink water or eat food. At last Andy said impatiently, 'Because we can – why else?'

'How pathetic you are!' I cried. 'And how cruel.'

'Well, you have the satisfaction of knowing you'll have saved one human life tomorrow,' replied Mr Lenchester, a twist of scorn on his lips, 'as we will now only have nine hundred and ninety-nine of our precious dogs for sale.

We are giving one to you now, totally free of charge.'

In all my fury about their plans for tomorrow I'd temporarily forgotten that I was to be their very first victim.

They'd both started moving closer to me. Andy was right in front of me now, with Mr Lenchester smiling, like a proud teacher behind her. Mrs Lenchester was hovering a bit uncertainly on the edges of this – her eyes looking everywhere but at me.

'Mrs Lenchester!' I called out. 'Please stop this.'

She got out a handkerchief as large as a sheet, blew her nose vigorously and declared, 'That's my weakness – too soft-hearted, always have been.'

'Soft-hearted?' I echoed disbelievingly. 'But you're going to let them do this.'

Mrs Lenchester shook her head. 'You foolish, foolish child. I could have helped you so much. You've thrown it all away, all your potential. Still, don't worry.' I looked at her, a desperate hope rising in me. 'I'll make us all a nice pot of tea for afterwards.' Then she thumped out.

Now Andy couldn't have stood much closer

to me if we'd been on a packed Underground train. And Mr Lenchester said to me in his dry, posh, unemotional voice, 'Come on, you must take the dog.' He could have been a doctor advising me to take my medicine until he added, 'Then at least you will be alive tomorrow.'

But without any memories – what kind of life was that? You lose your memories, you lose yourself. I'd never been more scared in my life. It took all my willpower not to scream. But I knew my screams would have as much effect on them as they would on a pint of milk. So I wouldn't give them that satisfaction.

'After you accept our present,' said Mr Lenchester, 'we will give you something to help you have a deep, refreshing sleep while we wait for the spell to work.'

'Then, at about eight o'clock,' said Andy, 'maybe even earlier, you will be free to go—' She stopped. She'd been about to say 'home', but of course I probably wouldn't know where my home was any more. So instead, she just said, 'Away.' She was pushing the dog at me now. But both my fists were tightly clenched. 'Come on, open your hands up,' said Andy.

I didn't answer but I could hear myself

breathing in and out. And then things happened very fast, as I suddenly flung myself down onto the musty red carpet. This took them both by complete surprise. So did my next action. Although I've never played rugby in my life I launched into a tackle at Andy's knees.

With a stunned, angry cry she went crashing forward, sending the dog flying out of her grip. It bounced off Rufus, who hissed in annoyance before streaking out of the room, and toppled onto the floor. I nearly cheered.

'The dog! Is it broken?' cried Mr Lenchester at once. That was his only concern.

Andy scrambled to her feet. 'No, no, it's all right.'

'Are you sure?' asked Mr Lenchester anxiously.

They were so busy examining it I saw my chance and shot to my feet. I'd actually reached the door before I staggered back. I'd forgotten the private army above my head. The bats were onto me so fast I barely saw them move. And reinforcements must have poured in from somewhere, as soon the bats were flying into my eyes, my hair and my nostrils. The stink was overwhelming and I began to cough and choke, while somehow still keeping my fists tightly closed. I couldn't even see to punch the bats away. Then I felt sharp fangs biting my neck. Instantly a searing pain surged through my body and I rocked forward dizzily. The carpet suddenly seemed to be rising up and hitting me in the face.

When I woke up I was lying face down on it. I had this wild sense of unreality then as I heard words being chanted right over my head. 'She is receiving this as a gift,' said Mr Lenchester.

'The spell should work now,' said Andy. 'She has accepted it.'

No, I haven't. *I haven't!*

'Just push it into her hand,' went on Andy. Every ounce, every wisp of strength I had was now directed at stopping that vile toy being forced on me. I kept my hands closed very tightly but I knew I couldn't hold out much longer. That was why at the same time I did something I've never done before – and never will again either.

I wished for a boy to rescue me: Marcus, ages ago, you were supposed to be outside. So why haven't you knocked on the door – done something, Marcus? I've never needed your help more urgently. Where are you?

Then I heard the most terrifying words ever. 'She's got the dog in her left hand,' said Andy. 'The spell is cast.'

I did feel something touching my hand. I couldn't see what it was as they curled my fingers around it, but I knew and I was too horrified even to react at first. I just froze. And then I heard someone pounding on the front door.

'Marcus!' I yelled out, as loudly as I could. 'Marcus!'

'Silence her now,' hissed Mr Lenchester.

And then . . .

And then . . .

I'm truly sorry, but I don't think I can keep my eyes open another second.

Thank you, reader, for keeping me company tonight.

You have helped me more than you'll ever know.

But I must leave it to Marcus to tell you the final part of my story.

For me, it all ends here.

# PART FOUR

*Marcus*

# CHAPTER TWENTY-ONE

## *Surprise Attack*

### 5.00 p.m.

Gracie and I tore all the way to Mrs Lenchester's cottage.

But before we could knock on her door a car sped towards us and a familiar voice yelled out, 'I thought I recognized you two.'

Of all the moments for Gracie's mum to turn up, this was positively the worst ever. 'Whatever were you running so fast for?' she went on, getting out of the car.

Recovering quickly, I said, 'Oh, you know us, we like to keep fit.'

'Since when?' demanded Gracie's mum.

'Since ten minutes ago,' I said. 'I'm supposed to have some exercise after my accident,' I added cunningly. 'Look – no stick!'

'What do you want, Mum?' demanded Gracie.

'What do I want? That's not very friendly.' Gracie's mum became quite huffy. 'I've driven all the way over here to take you home.'

'But didn't you get my message?' asked Gracie.

'No, I've been too busy to check—'

'Mum, I left you a message saying I was staying over at Marcus's house tonight.'

Her mum turned an amazed face to me. 'But I've just come from your house and your parents never said anything about it.'

'They've only just decided,' I said. 'They think Gracie is a good influence on me. The mad fools. Anyway, we mustn't hold you up. See you tomorrow.'

Even Gracie looked a bit shocked at the speed with which I was trying to get shot of her mum. But I was feeling more and more uneasy about Tallulah visiting Mrs Lenchester. Something wasn't right here. I just knew it.

'Can I drop you anywhere?' asked Gracie's mum.

'No thanks, we'll just carry on keeping fit,' I said.

'Well, don't exhaust yourselves, and I'll see you tomorrow then, Gracie.'

At last Gracie's mum got back in the car, but then she was ages turning the car round and I was becoming more and more impatient. When she'd finally gone, I hissed to Gracie, 'Let's really hammer on that deadly vampire's door now.' I marched up the path and thumped on the door with both fists. But no one came to answer.

'Can you hear anything at all?' I asked Gracie.

'I thought I heard someone yell out my name – but I couldn't be sure.'

We strained to hear any other noises – but there was nothing.

The late afternoon still shimmered with pale sunshine and I suddenly noticed Mrs Lenchester's cottage door had been painted recently. It all seemed so tranquil. Yet I was sure Tallulah was inside the silent cottage.

'Time for a surprise attack,' I said.

'You mean, we shape-change?' said Gracie.

'Exactly.'

Transforming into a bat is something every half-vampire can do, after a little bit of training. To us, it's just like riding a bike. The one essential is to find somewhere you can't be seen doing so as the last thing we want to do is alarm any humans. So we went to the river, which was, as we'd hoped, deserted.

'Quick as you can,' I said to Gracie.

Then we both strutted about on tiptoe – I always feel a bit silly doing this bit – while thinking about nothing at all.

I guess I must have found it hard to shut all my worries about Tallulah down, as Gracie had whooshed up in the air and started soaring around as a bat while I was still doing my very bad impersonation of a ballet dancer.

But finally I got off the ground as well and then two bats whirled off to Mrs Lenchester's chamber of horrors.

### 5.20 p.m.

I shall hate telling you most of what happened next, especially— But I'm jumping ahead.

Gracie and I shape-changed into bats and

194

were able to slip through Mrs Lenchester's back window.

'Never thought I'd be dropping into this rickety old cottage again,' I said. It was the smell I remembered first, a shut-up mustiness as if everything in here were old and dead. Then I heard the voices coming from the front.

'This place creeps me out,' said Gracie.

'If you want to wait here—' I began.

'Behave,' Gracie hissed back.

We flew in the direction of the voices and found ourselves in a room so tiny you could probably have fitted it into a large packing case. Our entrance attracted no attention from either of the two 'people' in the room, as other bats were already fluttering about like a permanent gang, and although they immediately began to flap about in consternation at our arrival it was only a reaction another bat would notice – to human ears it would just be a slight increase in the noise of their wings.

Mrs Lenchester and the oldest man I've ever seen were peering out of the window. 'I definitely saw them walking away,' said Mrs Lenchester.

'But they were so insistent knocking on that door,' quavered the old boy. 'I can't believe they would just go.'

They went on looking out of the window as if they were caught up in a siege. But where was their hostage? Where was Tallulah?

Leaving the confused bats behind us, Gracie and I flew off into a large, cluttered room I remembered very well. Tallulah was sitting on the large, green sofa, all alone save for a single bat right in the shadows of the ceiling. Her hands were tied up and there was a large hankie stuck over her mouth. She was shivering slightly as if the room were very cold (it was actually stiflingly hot) but her face was set in a mask of grim determination. Good old Tallulah, I thought. We'll be back. Then I whispered to Gracie, 'I think it's time for us to say hello to our hosts.'

'I really think you're right.'

We flew back into the tiny room, just as the old man was saying, 'We'll send two of them off to take a look around,' nodding at the bats. 'We need to know exactly where those abominations have gone.'

I looked at Gracie. In the blink of an eye we

both shape-changed back, and I announced, 'We're right behind you actually.'

'It's just a flying visit,' added Gracie.

Mrs Lenchester and the ancient geezer both whirled round and squinted at us in absolute consternation. Mrs Lenchester was spluttering, 'But how . . . did you get in here?'

'Dead easily,' I said. 'We did knock first but you didn't answer, which isn't very friendly.'

'Neither is tying a handkerchief over a guest's mouth,' said Gracie.

'Really kills the art of conversation,' I agreed. 'So we'll sort that out now.'

I don't think I ever saw a face turn as red with fury as that old geezer's did. Then I saw his rheumy old eyes fix on the bats. He was about to tell them to attack us when Mrs Lenchester said in a very low, warning voice, 'Remember – this is Marcus.'

'And don't you forget it,' I called cheerfully.

He wilted instantly. It was stupendous. Now I know why those superheroes were always so cool and calm: knowing you have tons of special powers to back you up certainly aids your confidence. I sauntered into the sitting room with Gracie right behind me, and Tallulah's eyes shone in total amazement and joy at seeing us. I bent down to remove the hankie from her mouth, while Gracie undid her arms.

And Tallulah said immediately, 'Your memory is back.'

'It sure is. It returned to me, would you believe it, in the Hinton Tea Rooms. I was catching up on my past when you rang. That's why I couldn't talk to you. I feel as if I haven't seen you for ages.'

'You haven't,' she replied at once. 'But how did you and Gracie – hi, Gracie, by the way – know I was here?' Then she answered her own question. 'My little sister.'

'That's right. But why *are* you here?'

'The deadly vampires are caught up in something bigger and darker than ever before,' began Tallulah. 'I had to find out what it was.'

'So you trotted along here all on your own.' I turned to Gracie. 'She's quite mad, you know. It's part of her charm.'

'And so are we,' said Gracie, 'hanging about chatting. Now we've found Tallulah, shouldn't we be trying to—'

The door opened and in shuffled Mrs Lenchester with the sweetest smile you've ever seen, and then she sat down on the couch beside Tallulah. You'd have thought from the rapt expression on Mrs Lenchester's face that she was settling down for a cosy chat next to her favourite granddaughter, not someone she'd just been holding hostage.

'Well, this is quite a reunion, isn't it?' she said. 'And you're all looking extremely well.'

'But you'll soon put a stop to that,' I said.

'Naughty boy,' chuckled Mrs Lenchester.

Then the old geezer glided in too. For such an elderly gent, he moved surprisingly smoothly. He didn't sit on the couch, though. He stood ramrod straight in the doorway, like a security guard. And all the time he stood there his eyes bored into me in a most unfriendly way, but he didn't say anything. He didn't dare. I so enjoyed that. In fact, I probably enjoyed that a bit too much.

But for now I was in control of things and that's why I moved into the centre of the room and announced, 'Isn't it great my memory's practically back to its gleaming self? And I am back at the peak of my form, delighting one and all once more. By the way, extremely civil of you, Mrs Lenchester, to have tea all ready for us.' I pointed at the tray of tea and biscuits on the table. 'Especially when you didn't even know we were dropping by. But how you expected Tallulah to drink her tea I really don't know. Anyway, you haven't introduced us to this young man.'

Mrs Lenchester murmured, 'I'm so sorry, this is my husband.'

For the first time since I'd arrived, I was taken aback. 'Your *late* husband?' I asked.

'Yes, he has returned to me,' said Mrs Lenchester.

'Are you – a ghost?' I asked.

'He hates you calling him that,' said Tallulah.

'I am certainly *not* a ghost,' said Mr Lenchester. 'And I must ask you not to get too close to me as I am allergic to the smell of abominations.'

'That's beyond nasty,' said Tallulah.

But I didn't want her enquiring too closely into why I'd been called an 'abomination' – after all, Tallulah still didn't know I was a half-vampire and I didn't want my secret getting out, even to her – so I said hastily, 'Well, you're a real fun machine, aren't you.'

Then we heard the back door open, followed by quick, confident footsteps, and in burst a very strange-looking woman.

'Ah, here's our very talented great-niece Andy,' said Mrs Lenchester, just as if she were hosting a little afternoon tea party.

'What are they doing here?' demanded Andy, frowning at us in an even more unfriendly way than Mr Lenchester.

Mrs Lenchester got up. 'A quick word, my dear.' She ushered her out of the room, after which we could just make out some frantic whispering. Mr Lenchester continued to glare malevolently at us from the doorway.

I smiled at him. 'Going anywhere nice for your holidays this year?'

Tallulah actually let out a burst of laughter. There's still nothing better in the world than making someone laugh – especially Tallulah. But Mr Lenchester just turned his head away from me as if I'd punched him.

'I don't think he can go anywhere,' I said.

Then Andy and Mrs Lenchester returned. And they stood on either side of Mr Lenchester.

Gracie suddenly pointed at Andy and cried, 'I know you – you're the one who sold me that horrible china dog.'

Andy's face widened into a horrible smile. Even now she couldn't miss an opportunity to revel in her own cleverness. 'And you well and truly fell for it, didn't you? We'd seen you sobbing your little heart out away on that bench, so we knew exactly how to hook you in.'

Gracie's face reddened.

'You foolish, gullible, love-struck monstrosity,' Andy went on. 'And any gift given with "love" always works strongly.' She sniggered.

I found a yell of anger pushing up through me. Especially when I saw how Gracie recoiled from Andy's very cruel words. But there was no point in arguing with deadly vampires. It was time to do something I'd been building up to for some time – to get us all out of here.

So I said, 'You've all made us feel so welcome, just like one of the family – although I'd so hate to be in your family – but we're leaving now.'

Immediately the tension in the room grew,

as I knew it would. Mr Lenchester and Andy seethed with fury and frustration. But they didn't say anything. They were still highly cautious at taking on a half-vampire with special powers. I turned to Tallulah. 'Will you walk out of here first?'

Tallulah didn't hesitate. 'I'll go with total pleasure.' But there was an odd quiver to her voice as she got up and began walking from the couch to the front door. Not a long journey at all. She was there in a few strides, standing right in front of the three of them, while the silence was as thick and heavy as the dust. If Tallulah walked safely past them and out of this house, then it was all over with the deadly vampires.

We'd defeated them for certain. The humiliation – the loss of pride – would destroy them.

No wonder the blood was thumping in my head as Tallulah said, 'Excuse me,' to Mrs Lenchester.

She didn't respond.

But then Mr Lenchester's voice cut through the silence like a gunshot. 'Stop!'

'Ignore him, Tallulah,' I urged. I was still

completely confident I could handle this situation.

But that's when three bats began to circle menacingly around Tallulah. They'd been so silent hovering above our heads that I'd half forgotten about them. But Mr Lenchester had obviously given them a small signal.

I looked up at them. 'Hey, come on, vamps. I'm your target.'

'I should warn you – they bite,' said Mr Lenchester.

'Look at me.' I grinned. 'I'm shaking.' Then I bowed to the bats. 'So you want to play, do you?'

# CHAPTER TWENTY-TWO

## *A Disaster*

Earlier, when Gracie had called me the 'local superhero', I'd lapped it up. My head had been swelling with pride.

But as the two bats swooped towards me, I felt this strange jolting sensation, like a massive shudder. My whole body shook with it.

Was it some kind of warning? *You love playing the role of a superhero, but you're not really one.* No, that was rubbish! I had the power all right, as I'd demonstrate now by seeing off those bats.

Suddenly there was a rush of stale air as

the bats landed on me. They immediately started digging into my neck. I turned round furiously and took in a huge breath of air, swinging my fists at them. It was beyond feeble. A new-born kitten could have fought them off better than me.

And then it was a multi-winged massacre as more and more bats, who must have been waiting outside or somewhere nearby for the signal, rushed at me in a mad whirl, screeching exultantly. I staggered back, struggling to rip them off me. But I couldn't. This was a complete and utter disaster.

All the time I was wondering what on earth was going on? It didn't make any sense. Then, quite suddenly, it did, as a last final memory just exploded in my head like a firework. And it wasn't a good one at all.

It was of me in Paris. Even though the course was still going on I'd had to leave, as I'd been chucked out. The reason was simple. The amazing special powers which I'd demonstrated in Great Walden against the deadly vampires had never once manifested themselves again. This happens occasionally. Special powers just flare up for a day or two, disappearing again almost immediately. Then it's as if they've hidden away behind an invisible wall, which can never be broken down.

And that's what had happened to me.

No wonder that was the very last thing I remembered. Anyone would rather forget a humiliation like that.

No one else – apart from my mum and dad, of course – knew. Not even Gracie. But that first day home with my parents struggling to put on a brave face was beyond grisly. That's why I went out on my bike late that afternoon . . . to try and escape from the news which I carried inside me like a lump of stone.

All this was flashing through my head as I tried to see off a mass attack of bats, failing so spectacularly that Gracie and Tallulah had to try and help me.

This wasn't how I'd planned things at all. But the horror wasn't over yet. For then Mr Lenchester said in his dry, raspy voice, 'Black widow.' I wondered why on earth he'd called that out – but soon I knew all right.

Something small and shiny black was

skittering up my leg. And then Mr Lenchester called out another name. It sounded like 'Hobo', and another spider landed straight on my stomach – the hairiest spider I'd ever seen in my life.

And then, like a mad, demented conjurer, Mr Lenchester couldn't stop. Next he called out, 'Jumping Spider', and immediately I saw in front of me a spider with huge eyes which jumped right up onto my face.

I so nearly shrieked out with terror then. Yes, all right, part of me knew it was just an illusion, but I could actually feel these spiders crawling over me, especially the jumping one, which was now on my nose. And you see, this was always my worst nightmare, to feel a horrible tickling sensation and then see a massive spider scuttling over me. And Mr Lenchester knew that, as deadly vampires can pick up your deepest fears within seconds of meeting you.

Meanwhile the bats had turned their attention to Tallulah and Gracie. That horrified me, even more than the deadly spiders. I'd come here to rescue Tallulah, and look at the result – Tallulah was in worse danger than ever, and now Gracie was caught up in it too!

I knew then that there was only one thing to do, much as I shrank from doing it. But I had no choice so I yelled out desperately, 'I give in!'

'I can't hear you,' crackled Mr Lenchester, who'd heard me all right – he just wanted a bit more grovelling.

'I give in!' was all he was going to get, but I really yelled it out this second time.

And it seemed that was enough.

Instantly all those gruesome spiders vanished. And just as if someone had pressed a switch the bats froze above our heads. Gracie, Tallulah and I retreated together into the corner of the room, right by the heavily curtained windows. 'I've messed up big time,' I said to them. 'And I'm really, really sorry.'

They both protested that it was absolutely fine and I was just a bit off my game today, that's all. But I felt now as far from a superhero as I ever had.

Then Mr Lenchester didn't so much walk as *ooze* towards us, his thin lips smiling faintly. 'This does not look good for our hero, does it? The White Knight has fallen off his horse and is unable to get up again. And I was told,' he went on, staring back accusingly at his wife for a moment, 'that this boy—'

'Rumours of his ability were obviously greatly exaggerated,' interrupted Andy contemptuously. 'He's as feeble as the rest of his species.'

'I can still hear you,' I said.

'Well, hear this,' said Mr Lenchester. 'Life is about one thing – *power*. Power rules the world. And you have just revealed to us that you haven't any. But don't worry – all we shall ask you to do is accept a present from us. Do we have any more ready?'

'Just two left, actually,' said Andy eagerly.

She left and Tallulah yelled out, 'No, no, no! You can't let them do that!'

# CHAPTER TWENTY-THREE

## *Indoor Lightning*

'They'll make you take a toy dog with black painted eyes,' she went on.

'Like the one I had before,' I said.

'The one I insisted on buying you,' added Gracie grimly.

'That car accident was just a red herring,' said Tallulah. 'It was the dog which had the spell on it, and whoever accepts it as a gift will lose their memory. Not immediately, but about twelve or fourteen hours later. Only these new dogs are far worse. They won't just wipe out a few months, they'll take away years and years . . .' Her voice broke, and she sounded choked suddenly.

'In fact, you'll be lucky if you remember your own name,' said Mr Lenchester in his dry, emotionless voice.

'But you can't do this!' cried Tallulah.

'I must disagree there,' said Mr Lenchester, totally in command now.

Mrs Lenchester went over and whispered something to him about the difficulty of keeping two more people in the cottage overnight.

'They will be asleep most of the time,' he replied, his sharp voice like drops of ice. 'And what else can we do? We have nine hundred and ninety-seven dogs, which arrived so late that we still have to spend most of tonight transforming them.'

Transforming them, I thought contemptuously. Infecting with their poison, more like.

'So we really can't waste any more valuable time on these abominations,' he said crisply.

Andy reappeared with two dogs in her hands. Mr Lenchester snatched them from her, then with Andy and Mrs Lenchester right behind him and his army of bats circling above he glided soundlessly towards us. His face was as stern and hard as a rock, his eyes like two black stones.

It was the most frightening face I'd ever seen.

For with no emotion at all this deadliest of assassins was going to rob us of years and years of our lives. I couldn't let this happen. I had to stop him. How? Right behind me was the window. I could throw myself against it. Smash my way out of here. That's what a superhero would do. But that wasn't me any more.

I could still try and protect Gracie, though.

I jumped in front of her.

'No, Marcus.' I could feel her hot breath on my neck.

'Yes,' I said firmly.

'Chivalrous to the very end,' said Mr Lenchester. His lips were actually twitching. He was laughing at us.

'Doesn't it make you want to puke?' cackled Andy. She really was as loathsome as her great-uncle.

I reached round to grab Gracie's hand and she seized hold of it. She was petrified –

and she wasn't the only one. I decided when the trio of deadly vampires got a bit nearer I'd fight them, and I wouldn't even try and call up my special powers since they'd obviously gone AWOL. I'd just set about having a massive scrap which I knew I couldn't win. But if I created enough of a diversion maybe Gracie and Tallulah might be able to make a break for it. It was a desperate plan but it was better than doing nothing.

At least I'd go down fighting.

I turned round to Tallulah. I offered to join hands with her too. But she shook her head firmly.

She was just bursting with rage on our behalf. 'I won't let you do this to them!' she suddenly shouted.

Andy gave a derisive cackle. And Mr Lenchester also permitted himself another small smile.

'This has got to stop now,' went on Tallulah. 'Do you hear me?'

'Deluded child,' muttered Mr Lenchester contemptuously.

I looked again at Tallulah. She was so mad with fury now that for a second I actually thought I could see sparks coming out of her eyes. Tallulah gets angry pretty regularly. But I'd never seen her like this. Then I noticed she had something in her hand too. Was she suddenly going to throw something at Mr Lenchester – and in the confusion could we try and make our escape?

Mr Lenchester was standing right in front of me now. 'We shall start with the broken-down White Knight,' he said, 'who positively leaks desperation. Accept this gift and you will feel no pain while our spell seeps into your mind and sucks up all your memories. So just—'

But now another voice shouted out, 'Go back into the darkness from whence you came!' It sounded so stern, so authoritative that at first I didn't recognize it as Tallulah's.

Then someone screamed, 'No, no!' It was Mrs Lenchester. And out of nowhere a bolt of jet-black lightning illuminated the entire room.

The lightning zigzagged through the air before wrapping itself around Mr Lenchester and lifting him right up into the air.

# CHAPTER TWENTY-FOUR

## *What Has Tallulah Done?*

Black smoke plumed around Mr Lenchester, still hanging in the air, as if by invisible strings. His hair was singed, his face and neck were purple, while the two dogs he'd been holding lay beneath him, both smashed in two.

Mrs Lenchester gaped at her husband, utterly horror-struck, and then turned on Tallulah. 'What have you done? What have you done?' She kept repeating the question like a demented parrot.

Gracie and I were also gaping at Tallulah in total amazement. 'You did that,' we chorused. 'But how?'

Tallulah's eyes were fixed in a look of total shock. 'She gave me a charm. I just—'

'I gave you that to take revenge on humans,' screamed Mrs Lenchester.

'You gave that creature a charm?' cried Andy.

'What charm?' I asked Tallulah.

Before she could answer Mrs Lenchester let out a shriek. Half of Mr Lenchester's body had just vanished – decayed away. The purple half of his face that was left was bursting with rage at his wife. 'You fool,' he croaked. 'You utter fool.' Only his voice had shrunk too, so it now sounded as if he were speaking from the bottom of a very deep well. 'You've destroyed everything . . . this is all your fault.' They were the very last words he hissed at his wife before the other half of his body decayed away too, leaving nothing behind but a few large particles of very withered-looking dust.

'Didn't you know Great-uncle wouldn't be able to resist the power of that charm?' yelled Andy at Mrs Lenchester. 'We had to gather up so many forces to enable him to materialize, and now you've helped a human destroy him for ever.'

'I know what I've done!' screeched Mrs Lenchester. 'Or what *you've* done,' she shouted at Tallulah. Her dark eyes seemed to have grown even blacker and sunk further into their sockets.

'I did warn you,' said Tallulah. 'And I had to stop him destroying my friends. But I didn't know what the charm could do.'

'Don't apologize,' I said to Tallulah.

'I'm not,' she said at once.

'You did a fantastic thing,' I went on.

'You saved us!' said Gracie. 'And now I really think we should leave and—' She never finished that sentence. Instead she let out a gasp. White slime had started drooling down Mrs Lenchester's chin, just as it had the last time we'd defeated her. A vampire's pride is so strong that when it loses that, everything is lost. Mrs Lenchester was already bent double, and now she started shrivelling away so quickly it was as if someone had pressed a fast-forward button, and within seconds all that was left of her was her mouth saying, 'My heart is crumbling to dust. It's all over.'

And then she was gone too.

'We really have seen the last of her now,' I said.

'Yes,' said Tallulah. But she didn't sound the least bit triumphant.

'That charm is dynamite,' I said.

'But why did she give it to you?' asked Gracie.

'She said I had special blood and was one of the golden ones,' said Tallulah very softly, 'and that with the aid of the charm I could do some magic. I think she was hoping she could persuade me to join her side, because she knew I'm not great with people.'

There was an eerie silence. The bats, who'd been fluttering above us, were now completely still again.

So was Andy, who was standing, head bowed, in the middle of the room.

I walked past her towards the door, nodding at Gracie and Tallulah to follow me. I said to Andy, 'You heard what Mrs Lenchester said. It's all over.'

Andy's head shot up. 'Why ever do you think that?'

# CHAPTER TWENTY-FIVE

## *The Worst News of All*

Craziness danced in Andy's normally expressionless eyes as she declared, 'I'm the one with the power here. We don't need those ancient relics.' It was touching to see how much she was missing her family. 'So the plan still goes ahead!' she yelled. Then she made this weird noise, a cross between a scream and a battle-cry, which filled the room.

'Make a run for it,' I said to the girls.

Tallulah faced me. 'I'm not going anywhere. I'll use the charm on the bats.' She reached forward, and just for a second grabbed my arm. 'Don't worry. I'm sure I can make it work again.'

Maybe it was because she sounded so determined, I don't know, but suddenly I was glowing with confidence. And I knew exactly what I had to do – direct the bats' attention towards me while Tallulah tried to activate that charm again.

Two vampire bats were already launching themselves at Tallulah's face. She held up one hand to protect herself while fumbling in her pocket for that charm.

And then something truly incredible happened. My whole body seemed to tingle and throb. It was as if some invisible power had seeped across the room to me. And it sparked me up like a jolt of electricity. The next moment I sent my fist hurtling towards those two bats who'd been terrorizing Gracie, and with one jab – no, truly I'm not exaggerating, that's all it took – sent both of them rocking across the room.

Cracking with confidence, I yelled, 'I'm back!' to Gracie and Tallulah, while sending another bat spinning away without even really trying.

My special power, which had gone missing for weeks, had – for some reason I couldn't fathom at all – wonderfully and spectacularly returned.

'Well done!' cried Gracie. Then she added, 'Look . . .'

A great bolt of fire had streaked from Tallulah's fingers and blasted its way towards the bat which had started attacking her. The bat was so shocked it shape-changed into its normal form – a very young vampire who didn't look any more than about sixteen or seventeen, with a really stunned expression seemingly fixed on his face. Then he exploded into thousands of pieces of dust, much of it falling onto Mrs Lenchester's couch.

'Hey, what a team!' I shouted at Tallulah.

'What a team!' she yelled back.

Then another vampire flew at me, shape-changing as he did so. He also looked young – and big and tough. He'd clearly decided to punch me into next week. A massive fist lunged towards me, but with just one hand (yes, all right, I was showing off a bit now) I not only hurled him away but sent him crashing against the wall. He slid to the floor, where he also exploded into a shower of dust.

I stared at him feeling like a footballer who, after being off form for most of the season, now can't stop scoring goals.

Tallulah was doing brilliantly too. But then Gracie yelled out a warning to her. Andy, who'd been watching us topple her young army with wild screeches of frustration, suddenly rushed towards Tallulah and started shaking her, like a rage-filled girl with a doll.

'Get off me,' wheezed Tallulah, who really hadn't been expecting this kind of attack.

And then I saw what Andy was up to. She was trying to swipe the charm out of Tallulah's grip. I charged over, but Tallulah's left hand had already started twisting about, sending a fireball flying right into Andy's stomach. Andy immediately recoiled as deep red flames totally engulfed her.

Then a howl tore through the air – the most rage-filled howl I've ever heard. It was actually like someone shouting a curse. And it really scared me.

Andy didn't shrivel into particles of dust. Instead, it was just as if she'd been gobbled up by some invisible creature, as one moment she was there, and the next

223

she'd gone. Her army of vampires had all disappeared too.

'We did it,' I said.

'You two were fantastic,' said Gracie. 'I only wish I'd remembered my autograph book.'

'Don't worry, it won't go to our heads,' I laughed. 'Well, not mine. I mean, I was rubbish earlier.'

'That's very true.' Gracie grinned. 'Still, you've made up for it now.'

Then we sank down onto the couch, sending dust – deadly vampire dust – flying everywhere. We were all exhausted.

'There's just one last thing to do,' said Tallulah in a low, quiet voice.

Gracie and I looked at her questioningly.

'We've got to find and destroy another toy dog. Bit of a downer really,' she went on, giving an odd little laugh. 'But you see, just before you two arrived, they forced me to accept one as a horrible sort of present.'

'You – you had to take one,' I stuttered, while Gracie's mouth was rounded in an O of total horror.

'Big pain, I know,' said Tallulah, so casually it made her news all the more shocking.

224

'Funny thing is, I never thought of using the charm then. I was too busy trying to fight my way out. I did do rather a good rugby tackle on Andy, sending her flying – but I dropped the china dog too.' She sighed heavily. 'I hoped I had smashed it, but no such luck. So back they all came – a mass attack.' Her voice fell away. 'I didn't stand a chance. I must have passed out for a few seconds, and when I woke up they were wrapping my hand around the dog and chanting stuff over me about how I'd accepted this gift and apparently that's enough for the spell to work.' She went on, 'Didn't you wonder why they only tried to force two dogs on us and why there wasn't one for me?'

I should have wondered, but I'm not sure I even noticed then. Too busy worrying about myself, I suppose.

'But come on, don't look so tense.' Tallulah was trying to cheer us up. 'And there is one bit of good news. After they'd forced the dog onto me, Andy took it away again to stop me trying to smash it up if I woke up. She definitely went into the kitchen and I'm sure I heard the click of a cupboard . . .'

'We'll find it,' I said at once. We tore into the kitchen, flinging open every single cupboard. Each one was crammed with tons and tons of stuff, including what must have been at least forty teapots as well as rows and rows of cups. But there was no sign of a china dog.

We carried on maniacally searching, throwing stuff everywhere. 'It's got to be here,' I said, convinced it would be.

But it wasn't.

Then Gracie said, 'Maybe Andy took it next door.'

'Come on, then,' I said. We sped round to the other cottage. The door swung open. An ominous sign, I thought. Either the vampire had already vacated her home, or for some reason she wanted us to wander in here. But I didn't say any of this.

In contrast to Mrs Lenchester's, this had hardly anything in it at all. It was mainly just plants – they were everywhere – and paintings of some deeply gloomy land-scapes.

We were searching frantically in here when a howl erupted from somewhere just behind us. It was exactly like the howl we'd heard

226

when Andy went up in flames. We twisted our heads.

'No, I'm not behind you,' said Andy's voice. 'But my voice carries wonderfully well. I just wanted to let you know . . . you'll never find that dog. I've made certain of that.'

'But you've lost!' I shouted. 'So what use is it to you now?'

'That dog is my small but totally lethal act of revenge!' cried Andy, her voice getting higher and more screechy all the time. 'Happy hunting . . .'

# CHAPTER TWENTY-SIX

## *The Discovery*

### 6.20 p.m.

We went on looking for the toy dog, just in case Andy had been lying. But we never found it. Finally we trailed outside.

At least it was a relief to be away from the stale, heavy clamminess which hung over both cottages and we breathed in gulps of fresh air.

'I suppose we'd better tell my parents about all this,' I said as we headed home. I wasn't looking forward to that at all. 'There's bound to be an antidote to your spell,' I said to Tallulah. 'And they'll know what it is. I mean, that's what parents are for, isn't it? Knowing things.'

Before she wondered what my parents might know that hers didn't – especially about spells from deadly vampires – I realized it would be best if I saw them on my own. Well, I had a lot to tell them. So I left Tallulah with Gracie in the sitting room and headed for the kitchen, where Mum and Dad were studying the plans for their new units.

They were in such a good mood I almost felt sorry for them. Then I rattled through the day's events. When I mentioned how Mrs Lenchester was back and Gracie and I had followed Tallulah into her cottage, a heavy sigh filled the air and I really thought Dad was going to explode with anger. He just managed to restrain himself while I thought, I've got something far, far worse to tell them than that.

Of course all the good stuff about my memory shooting back and my special powers making a return appearance were totally overshadowed by the truly terrible news about Tallulah and the memory spell she was now under.

'That poor, poor girl,' said Mum when I'd finished. Mum has never been very keen on Tallulah. For a start, she thinks she's too interested in half-vampires and vampires – and leads me into trouble. But now she was so totally shocked and horrified about what had happened to her – they both were – it seemed to wipe out everything else, including having a big moan at me.

'But there are ways of breaking that spell, aren't there?' I said, looking at them hopefully.

'I don't know any.' Mum's voice was barely a whisper.

'Oh, I told Tallulah you would. But what about the charm? Surely that will protect her? It's incredibly powerful, you know.'

'I'm not sure it can protect against one of their spells.' Mum turned to Dad, who was standing motionless in thought in the middle of the room. 'What do you think?'

Dad didn't answer at first. His face was so still and thoughtful and sad that it alarmed me. 'Your mum and I are a bit out of our depth,' he said slowly at last. 'But actually we had been consulting' – he lowered his voice – 'half-vampire experts about your accident—'

'I knew it,' I interrupted. 'I knew you were only pretending to be so relaxed about it all.'

Dad sighed, and then admitted, 'From the start we feared your accident might have been deliberate.'

'Set up by deadly vampires,' I said.

Dad nodded. 'But we didn't want to worry you.'

And then Jean-Paul came to see us,' said Mum. 'You remember him now?'

'Of course I do,' I said. 'He was in my class in Paris, and yes, he turned up selling flowers one day, didn't he? Only I didn't recognize him then.'

'He was so desperate for your memory to return he tried everything. One night we even thought we saw him standing outside your bedroom window, waving his fingers around as if he were casting a spell,' said Mum.

'But why didn't he just come round here and talk to me?' I asked.

'Because we'd forbidden him to do that,' said Mum.

'Forbidden him!' I was stunned.

'He told us,' said Dad, 'that he had to see you very urgently as Mrs Lenchester was back and planning something big, and needed you to help him stop her. We said that was out of the question until your memory returned. We had a very small hope it might come back naturally. And then Jean-Paul disappeared – we think he must have given up and gone back to France. But as the days went by . . .'

'You became more and more convinced I was under a spell,' I said.

'Yes.' The word seemed to be torn out of Dad. 'So we've been discussing your case with experts. They were due to see you tomorrow actually. So now I will get their advice on this new problem.' He turned to Mum. 'Just keep things as normal as you can here while I'm doing that.'

Dad strode past the table with all the new kitchen plans on it – that was totally forgotten now – while Mum started getting the meal ready. She called Tallulah and Gracie in and chatted to them about everything except what had happened today.

Mum also switched on every radio and television we had. I'd never known the house so noisy. And she actually encouraged us to go and play some computer games. I knew what Mum was doing – she wanted us to distract ourselves – and it sort of worked.

Dad was gone for ages. Then he and Mum had this brief whispered conversation. After which they invited Tallulah to stay over for the night.

'There's plenty of space in our spare room for you two girls,' said Mum.

Tallulah agreed at once. Then she and Mum rang up Tallulah's parents. At first they were – well, more than a bit surprised. But Mum explained that we were having a sleep-over with Gracie here too – and Tallulah was really enjoying herself. So in the end they said how pleased they were that Tallulah was making new friends. And it was very kind of my parents to invite her.

Then Dad said, as casually as he could, that it would be best if we just relaxed tonight and we'd deal with whatever faced us tomorrow.

Tallulah looked grave but didn't say

anything else. She seemed lost in thought for a while, though. What was she thinking?

If I'd been in Tallulah's situation I'd be saying to myself, Why did I ever go to Mrs Lenchester's cottage on my own? If only I hadn't . . . *If only*. I'd make my head ache with those two words.

Was that what Tallulah was doing? Or was she thinking about the abilities she never knew she had until now, and that magic charm? And how, if her memory disappears, she'll never really get a chance to use them?

And then there was one of those long silences when no one is quite sure what to say until Mum and Dad started acting all lively. Dad began telling us – for no reason in particular – about this beard party he'd gone to as a teenager where everyone – even the girls – had to wear stick-on beards. The beards felt ever so hot and itchy and regularly fell into the drinks. We all – including Tallulah – were laughing now and firing questions about this daft party.

And that's how we started playing a game called 'let's pretend everything is normal'.

## 11.30 p.m.

You know that game I mentioned? We ended up playing it for three hours.

We all watched three whole episodes of this reality show about kids getting ready for a school prom – something my parents would never have done normally (they are very snooty about all reality shows, actually). But tonight Tallulah was saying how she'd hate to go to a school prom: 'That's where fun goes to die.' But Gracie was arguing that they seemed good fun and just made everyday life a bit special.

And I don't think either Gracie or Tallulah felt anything like as strongly about school proms as they were letting on. They were just making sure there weren't any sudden frightening stretches of silence.

We all were.

Finally Gracie announced she was 'dead tired' (she looked shattered, actually). So Mum disappeared with her to get the spare room ready. Dad also left to make still more phone calls. And Tallulah and I were on our own for the first time since I'd arrived home.

I stared at her sitting opposite me and

then said, 'If I were you now I'd be in such a horrible mood.'

'Oh, I'm always in a horrible mood.'

'I remember.' I grinned briefly and then said, 'Tallulah—'

'Just don't ask me how I feel.' Her chin went right up as she said this.

'How insulting – as if I could be so unoriginal. No, I was just going to say, I like your style.'

Tallulah immediately bristled a bit. She never took compliments easily – not even now. I hurriedly continued, 'I think – in fact, I'm certain – you'll be just fine tomorrow. That charm will protect you for a start. No spell's going to get past that, is it?'

'Hope not,' she murmured lightly.

'But on the random off-chance that some-thing weird and totally depressing does happen tomorrow' – I paused, as there was so much I wanted to say, but it was impos-sibly hard to express any of it, especially with Tallulah frowning away at me all the time – 'well, I just want you to know, I'll never let you down.'

'You'd better not.' There was a shake in her voice for the first time that night.

'And if the worst happens, which it won't,' I said jerkily, 'I'll tell you stories about all the mad things you did before.'

'And I'll still be me, somehow, won't I?'

Tallulah was looking right at me now. 'Of course you will,' I said, practically shouting for some reason. 'And you won't get rid of me, whatever happens. I'll still be there, helping you make some new, totally brilliant memories.'

Tallulah seemed as if she were about to say something else, but in the end she just looked away and said quickly, 'You know what, I'm dead tired too.'

'It's a result of talking to me.'

'Probably.' She got up. 'See you tomorrow then, Marcus.'

'Yeah, see you tomorrow, Tallulah.' Then, just as she was going, I added, 'Hey, I meant to tell you before, I really like your boots.'

Tallulah briefly turned round. 'Would you believe – a present from my little sister.'

'Just be careful when you wear them that you don't frighten the traffic.'

Tallulah laughed – and even now I felt a little glow when she laughed at one of my jokes – and then she was gone.

## 11.50 p.m.

I'd been sitting downstairs on my own for a few minutes when Mum appeared, looking for that pad she'd bought recently, as Tallulah wanted some paper. 'I expect,' said Mum, 'she wanted to scribble a message to her family, just in case . . .'

Then her voice fell away.

## 12.05 a.m.

I was going upstairs to have one last chat with Tallulah when Mum stopped me. She said both girls were asleep already – which really surprised me – and I wasn't on any account to disturb them.

## 12.50 a.m.

I'm sitting downstairs with my parents. The television is still on, though not as loudly, so as not to disturb Gracie and Tallulah. This incredibly long evening is a kind of torment for all three of us. We knew there was no point in going to bed as we couldn't sleep, and half-vampires stay up later than humans anyway. But it was so hard to keep the conversation going. We did discuss why my special powers had leaped back so suddenly. 'They probably needed a catalyst,' Dad said.

'You know what a catalyst is?' Mum asked me.

'Yeah, sure, it's . . . well, a catalyst makes things react faster.'

'That's right,' said Mum. 'And we think either Gracie – who has picked up some of your telepathic messages in the past – or Tallulah could be your catalyst – without even realizing it, of course.'

'But one of them is sending you a powerful gift,' went on Dad.

'Wow, wow, wow,' I said. 'But which of the girls is it?'

Then I thought of something. 'The first time I tried to use my special powers at Mrs Lenchester's today, nothing happened.' Before they could reply, I rushed on, 'But my memory still hadn't fully returned then.'

'Exactly,' said Mum. 'You weren't ready. You weren't receptive—'

'But later,' I interrupted excitedly, 'Tallulah briefly touched my arm. It was over in a flash. But right away I felt stronger, taller somehow. And then all my special powers just surged back. She's the one, all right. Tallulah's my catalyst.'

'We wouldn't have considered her at all before,' Mum replied slowly. 'But Mrs Lenchester gave her the charm for just one reason – she recognized Tallulah had special, magical blood.'

'And that's extremely rare in a human,' said Dad.

'Which means that when I'm near Tallulah my own special powers are much more likely to flare up?' I said.

'Exactly,' said Mum.

'And if I'd taken good old Tallulah to Paris – my special powers would probably have shown themselves there?'

'You could never have taken Tallulah to Paris on a course for' – Mum lowered her voice – 'half-vampires. But,' she added, totally un-expectedly, 'we might be able to trust Tallulah more than most other humans.'

Now I tell you that was a massive conces-sion from my mum. But I'd noticed a major shift in both their attitudes to Tallulah tonight. And it wasn't only because she had vampire blood. They'd been dead impressed by the way she'd just got on with things, despite the truly terrible fate which is hanging over her, hanging over all of us, like a heavy fog.

### 2.15 a.m.

I'm in bed now with a hot chocolate beside me to help me sleep (it's the third one I've had tonight) and Mum said that on no account was I to bother the girls. 'You'll only make tonight harder for Tallulah,' said Mum.

I had no intention of 'bothering' the girls. But I did stand outside their room – listening. I could hear that rhythmic breathing which usually means someone is asleep. Just in case it was only Gracie though, I hissed, 'Hey, Tallulah,' twice – but got no answer. So hopefully she was asleep too. I hope so. Or maybe she just didn't want to talk to anyone.

I couldn't blame her if that were the case. I mean, to wake up with all your memories gone – that would be like being far away from your home and friends all the time. Losing six months of memories had been painful enough for me, but this would be far worse. I just had to hope with all my heart that somehow this wouldn't happen to Tallulah.

I suppose really I'm hoping for a miracle.

### 5.30 a.m.

Never thought I'd fall asleep tonight, but
I must have done, only to be woken up by
the sound of someone moving about on the
landing. I shot out of bed. It was Dad. He said
he was going back to Mrs Lenchester and
Andy's cottages to check if they really had
gone (one of the half-vampire 'experts' asked
him to do this) and to have one last look for
that toy dog. I asked if I could go with him.
We're leaving now.

### 6.30 a.m.

Dad drove quickly to the cottages, which like
everywhere else at this time seemed sunk in
sleep. Plants in both gardens gleamed and
glistened with dew.

But even now, with nothing to break the
stillness, a sense of menace seemed to linger
here. 'I'll go in first,' said Dad, pulling back
his shoulders.

I followed him into Andy's cottage. Dad
thought this was where the dog was most
likely to be. The door was slightly ajar. Would

Andy suddenly materialize again? We prowled around warily. I also wondered if Dad and I were suddenly discovered here if we would be mistaken for burglars. But right now that was the least of our worries.

Anyway, we didn't find anything there. And Andy didn't pop up either. We moved on to Mrs Lenchester's. Her door was closed but not locked. It seemed such a slim hope we'd find the dog here as we'd hunted around so carefully yesterday. The smell was so much worse here now. It reminded me of rotting seaweed.

Dad was opening and closing cupboards in the kitchen while I was just wandering around the living room when I felt something catch on my shoe, like a nail or ... Quite absentmindedly I picked it off and was about to fling it away. Then I stopped.

'No, it can't be ...' I whispered.

# CHAPTER TWENTY-SEVEN

## *A Letter Which I Should Never Have Seen*

I stared at it. And for a few seconds I couldn't do anything, my heart was pounding so furiously. Then I vaulted over to Dad. 'Hey . . .'

'Keep your voice down,' he began. Then he saw how worked up I was.

'Look!' I was still shouting. I couldn't help it. Never, ever can the discovery of a small piece of a toy dog's tail have aroused such excitement.

Dad grabbed it from me while I gabbled on, 'Tallulah said she thought she'd smashed the dog. And she had. Only it was such a tiny bit of damage they never noticed. But it's enough to break the spell, isn't it?'

Dad didn't answer at first, just stared at it. 'Oh yes, it's enough,' he said finally. 'But are you positive it's from . . . ?'

'Practically positive,' I said. 'The other two dogs broke right in two. No, it's got to be the one Tallulah held.' Dad handed the tiny part of the dog's tail back to me very carefully as if it were a piece of gold.

But actually, it was far more valuable than that.

### 7.20 a.m.

When we got home Mum and Gracie were both downstairs in the kitchen. Mum was in her dressing gown but Gracie was dressed.

I just floated in there and announced, 'Feast your eyes on this,' while holding up that piece of the dog's tail. I didn't need to say any more. Both Mum and Gracie instantly knew what it meant.

'Oh, Marcus, way to go!' yelled Gracie, while Mum just shook her head as if she couldn't believe it. We were all beaming at each other.

Then Dad said he'd better ring and cancel the experts he had standing by – something he was delighted to do.

He and Mum went off while I asked Gracie, 'Is Tallulah awake yet?'

'She wasn't when I crept out.'

'Well, I'll wake her right now with the brilliant news,' I said.

'Just before you do,' said Gracie, speaking very quickly, 'I couldn't possibly go home before I knew, but now I do and it's totally brilliant. So I'll be off.'

I stared at her. 'What, now?'

'Yes.'

'But why so early?'

'I told you how I had a small role in the school play, didn't I? Well, I was so tired I never checked my messages last night, but there's a whole load of them saying the girl playing the lead role has had to drop out because – to be honest I'm not sure why – but anyway, they want me to come to an urgent rehearsal because they think I'm the one to replace her.'

'Of course you are. In fact, they should have given you the lead role in the first place.'

She smiled. 'Thanks, Marcus. Anyway, I know it's going to be a lot of work, but I can't wait.'

'Well, book me a ticket for the first night.'

'Of course.'

'Front row.'

'Where else?' She hesitated. 'But the thing is, I'm going to be so incredibly busy that I probably won't be able to see you for a while.' Then she leaned forward and kissed me lightly on the top of my head, just as if she were dismissing me. 'Take care of yourself, Marcus.'

'Take care of myself? I'm not sure if I like the sound of that.'

She just smiled and said, 'You go and see Tallulah.' And before I could reply she'd turned away from me and started phoning her mum.

I hesitated for a moment, then tore up the stairs to where Tallulah was sleeping. Amazingly she was still asleep. 'Wake up,' I hissed, 'as I've got the best news ever.'

She still didn't stir. Then I noticed on the table by the bed was that writing pad Mum had given her. There were pages and pages of writing. It looked like Tallulah had been writing everything that happened to her since she came back from the sanatorium. And fixed on top of the pad was a sheet of paper which began: *Dear Marcus*.

I picked it up. It said:

If you're about to read this then it can only mean the worst has happened. Everything I wanted to say is here in this pad – except – well, as I shall never get another chance, I want you to know that I think you're the best human in the universe. As I only like about four humans it's not exactly a massive compliment. And if you ever tell anyone else I wrote that, I'll kill you – and that's a promise . . .

'Just what do you think you are doing?' demanded a highly indignant voice from the bed. Tallulah was sitting bolt upright in bed, blinking groggily at me.

'I'm just reading—'

'Well, you had no business reading that.'

She shot forward and snatched it out of my hand. 'It's totally private.'

'So why's it got "To Marcus" on it, then?'

She squinted down at it. 'You still should have asked me first.'

'Look,' I said, 'I'm not going to wake you up to ask if I can read a note which says "To Marcus" . . .'

'Don't tell me what I wrote, I do remember.' Then she stopped and looked at me. '*I remember!* But – but how?' She was shocked, disbelieving.

'That's what I raced up here to tell you before you bit my head off.' I grinned at her. 'Dad and I went back to the cottages and we – well, me actually – found this.' I held up that tiny piece of the toy dog's tail. 'So you did break it *and* the spell after all. And Andy's hidden the rest of that dog away for nothing.'

Tallulah gaped at me. She needed a couple of attempts before she could say anything at all. Finally she said softly, incredulously, 'We won, Marcus.' Then we hugged each other so hard until Tallulah suddenly broke away from me and announced, 'OK, I've got to get up now.'

'No, you haven't. You've just been through a really shattering—'

'But I don't want to lie here thinking about it, do I? Now, 1 bet you and your dad didn't think to check the shed at Mrs Lenchester's?'

'We were rather busy at the time.'

'I'm not blaming you – I'm just saying we need to make sure none of those dogs had their eyes painted black and could be used by other deadly vampires. We also need to check Andy really has gone. I have my doubts. And find out if Rufus is still hanging about. And after that we'd better go and see Herbert Cheshire. He really should know just what's been going on in his shop and then—'

'No, no more.'

She grinned at me. 'I'll probably send you crazy by the end of the day.'

'Probably,' I agreed. 'I can't wait.'